RESTORING THE REPENTANT

A SPECULATIVE FICTION NOVELLA

THE NEXT HIGH PRIEST SERIES
BOOK 9

PETER DEHAAN

To all who seek restoration and all who help them on their journey.

CONTENTS

Restoring the Repentant 1

1. A Dubious Outing 3
2. Who Is Patrice? 11
3. Chloe's News 17
4. Emma's Gaffes 27
5. Emma's Progress 33
6. Hugs 39
7. No Hugs 43
8. Organ Music 51
9. Barney's Battle 59
10. Family Matters 67
11. Road Trip 73
12. A Fateful Visit 79
13. Sunday Revelations 87
14. Monday Meetings 95
15. The VIP Donor Club 105
16. Barney's Baby Step 113
17. Preparing for the Donors 121
18. Dealing with the Donors 125
19. Diane's Adventure 131
20. Philanthropy 141
21. The Email 149
What's Next? 157
The Curious Gift 159

About Peter DeHaan 165
Fiction Books by Peter DeHaan 167

RESTORING THE REPENTANT

In a world just like ours . . . only different.

May the Lord's love shine upon you, fill you with peace, and overflow with joy as you go forth to help those who hurt, proclaim the good news across the land, and restore to fellowship all who repent. -History 79.146.

1

───────

A DUBIOUS OUTING

Emma waited for Jennifer by her teacher's car. They had an unusual relationship, but it worked. At first Jennifer was Emma's food server, but Emma soon changed that. Now Jennifer was Emma's instructor at their microschool in the mornings. The rest of the time they interacted as friends, even though Jennifer was ten years older. Overshadowing all this was the reality that Emma was also Jennifer's boss—actually her boss's boss. Despite all this, they got along just fine.

Emma groaned. She didn't want to do this. But she had to. She shifted from her right foot to her left and back again.

She'd only waited a few minutes when David's

sports car roared up. From the passenger seat, Jennifer leaned over and gave her boyfriend a quick kiss. She jumped out and headed to her car as David rumbled away.

"I still can't believe they arrested the Prime Minister." Jennifer shook her head. "You and Scarlett were brilliant in uncovering her conspiring to kill you . . . along with all her other crimes."

"Scarlett did the investigative reporting," Emma said. "I merely told her what the Sovereign had told me."

"Your humble spirit is one of the many things that draw people to you," Jennifer said. "First Barney Clark was arrested for trying to kill you. Then the seven rebellious priests were arrested for receiving stolen Temple funds. And now the Prime Minister." Jennifer chuckled. "People should realize now that if they get in your way, you'll take them out."

"I turn them over to the Sovereign for judgment," Emma said. "It's not my job to punish."

Jennifer unlocked her car and climbed in. Emma walked around to the other side and slid in. Jennifer started the engine and drove toward their destination.

"Are you sure you want to do this?" the teacher asked the student.

Emma considered her answer before speaking. In truth, she didn't. "Yes." She confirmed her answer with a decided downward tip of her head.

"So I can't talk you out of it?"

"Nope."

"Have you discussed this with anyone?" Jennifer asked.

"Hernandez said it was a bad idea," Emma replied.

"Given that he's your head of security, that makes sense. What about Frederick?"

"He said I didn't have to do it and wouldn't blame me if I didn't."

"That makes sense too. As your executive admin, he'd need to deal with any fallout. What about Joshua?"

"Didn't ask," Emma said. "I knew he'd be against it but would insist on tagging along anyway."

"You should be happy to have a boyfriend who wants to protect you and keep you safe."

"I am. I really am. But sometimes he's too protective."

"Not to be critical," Jennifer said, "but a failure

to communicate has caused problems with you two in the past. Like when he went undercover to find out where the prisoners were being held when you didn't want him to."

Emma groaned. "I ordered him not to do it. I can't believe I played the High Priestess card on him. Then I ignored him for a couple of days."

Jennifer was right. Every problem in Emma and Joshua's short relationship was because of a lack of communication—mostly on Emma's part. She'd need to do better. But now that she'd already committed to this dubious meeting, it was too late to correct her mistake—this time.

Jennifer continued her gentle counsel. "Don't forget that David and I spent three years away from each other, all because we didn't communicate. If you hadn't intervened and gotten us back together, we'd still be apart today."

"I guess it's easier to see other people's problems than my own," Emma said. "Let me know the next time you see me messing up."

"You can count on it," Jennifer said. "One more question. What did Gabe say about all this? He's your spiritual mentor, after all."

"At first, he wasn't in favor of it either," Emma

said. "But once he knew the Sovereign told me to do it, he was completely behind me."

"Wait just a minute! The Sovereign told you to do this? You should've led with that."

"Gabe's praying for me right now. That I'll have the strength to do what the Sovereign told me to do."

"I'll also pray for you during your meeting."

Emma shifted in her seat, not that she was uncomfortable—at least not in a physical sense. She changed the subject. "How have things been going with you and David?"

"We couldn't be better." Jennifer let out a happy sigh. "I did as you suggested and proclaimed that the Sovereign's Divine Spirit fill him. And it happened! I still don't understand it, but we're now at the same place spiritually."

"So you're ready to get married?"

"Most definitely." Jennifer's head bobbed with excitement. "We really like how you officiated Ashley and Topher's wedding on Saturday. It was simple yet meaningful. We agree with your focus on marriage as a lifelong commitment made in front of family, friends, and the Sovereign."

"The Holy Text says the Sovereign hates divorce. The key to a good marriage is to be faithful and commit to push through the hard times together." Emma grinned, a response that started in her mind and bloomed on her face. "And, of course, good communication."

"Before we pick a date, we'd like a married couple to do some pre-wedding mentoring with us," Jennifer said. "Do you have any suggestions?"

"Great idea." Emma searched her mind, thinking aloud. "None of the priests are married . . . yet. That's not an option. Olivia has the training, but she's single too. I suspect some of our married staff would be open to mentoring you, but I'm not sure who to ask. Although . . ."

"Although who?" Jennifer asked.

"Maybe my parents," Emma said. "They have a great relationship. I've learned a lot from watching them. I'll email them."

"Wouldn't a text be quicker?"

"Mom prefers email."

By the time Emma had sent the message, Jennifer had arrived at their destination. She pulled into the prison parking lot and stopped in front of the visitors' entrance.

Buoyed by her confidence in the Sovereign, Emma strode through the doors, cleared security, and marched to the counter. "I'm here to see Barney Clark."

2

WHO IS PATRICE?

The woman at the counter typed on her keyboard and shook her head. "Sorry. Barney Clark isn't accepting visitors."

"He'll see me. Tell him Emma Barlow is here."

The woman's attention snapped to Emma. She scrutinized the High Priestess. "My apologies, My Lord." The woman gave a respectful downward tip of her head.

"Please call me Emma and treat me like everyone else. But will you double-check?"

The woman made a couple of quick mouse clicks and gasped as she studied the screen. "Again, my apologies . . . Emma. Your name is indeed on the exception list. So is Gabriel Cruz."

"He's my mentor," Emma explained. "I didn't know, but it doesn't surprise me either."

"Please print your name, date, and time on the visitor sheet. Then sign it." The woman slid a clipboard to Emma. Then she gestured to her right. "You can wait over there. The guards will get the prisoner and escort him to the visitor area. It normally takes about fifteen minutes, but I'll put a rush on it for your sake."

"No hurry," Emma said. "I can wait."

Emma took a seat and pulled out her phone to text Gabe that he was on Barney's pre-approved visitor list. When finished, she shoved the device back into her pocket and closed her eyes.

In seemingly no time, the woman interrupted her. "Emma," came a gentle whisper. "Is everything okay?"

Emma's eyes popped open. "I was just praying."

"Sorry for interrupting you. He's in the visitors' area and ready to see you." The woman pointed to a set of double doors behind Emma. "I'll buzz you through."

Bolstered by the Sovereign's confidence and the knowledge that this was an act of obedience, Emma stood and strolled through the doors, which opened as she approached, with her shoulders back and her head held high. The meeting room held nine white tables, each with two folding chairs, one on each side.

Barney sat at the center table, dressed in his prison garb. Bright orange was not his color. With a pleased smirk plastered on his face, he leaned back and put his hands behind his head. His eyes twinkled.

Emma considered standing at the table to glare down at him. She also thought about offering to shake his hand. She did neither. Instead, she sat in the table's other chair, facing him.

"I knew you'd come crawling back to me to beg for help. As always, I am ready to assist. As I confirmed with Hernandez, PM stands for Prime Minister."

Emma shook her head. "I'm not here because I need help. I'm here because the Sovereign sent me."

The grin faded from Barney's face, and he brought his hands to rest on the table. "Not another word to me about the Sovereign or your delusional religion. I know you have questions, and I have answers." A hint of a smile again played on his lips. He gave Emma a smug wink.

Emma recoiled on the inside, but on the outside

she remained calm. "The Sovereign told me you're a hurting man. I'm here to help you—not the other way around."

Barney shook his head. "I don't need your help. As soon as Patrice pardons me, I'll be out and ready to resume my life. It will either be at your side or in opposition to you. You decide."

Emma scrunched up her face. "Patrice?"

"Patrice Overton. You know, the Prime Minister.

Now it was Emma's turn to shake her head. "The Prime Minister's been arrested, so don't expect a pardon."

"What!" Barney jerked back. "We get no news here, and we can't access the internet. What's she accused of?"

"For conspiring with you in the death of the former high priest, and for the attempt to kill me. Among other things, there are also corruption charges for colluding with G. S. Acerman about some serious campaign finance violations."

Barney's shoulders sagged. "I can't believe it!"

"Her career in politics is over," Emma said, "and she's sure to spend the rest of her life in prison —just like you."

The pair sat in silence. Emma waited for Barney

to speak. At last he did. "Be that as it may, you still need my help."

Emma shook her head. "No. You need mine."

"What about dealing with the major donors?"

"I don't care about donations. The Sovereign will provide what we need."

A bit of bravado returned to Barney's face. "I suspect you'd appreciate knowing my computer password."

"It's 'Montgomery'." Emma grinned. "The Sovereign told me. I also know the password for your secret email account with the Prime Minister."

Barney gulped but then recovered from his shock. "There's next to nothing for you to see. So it doesn't matter. I don't care if you can access it."

"Did you realize that one feature in the deluxe plan you signed up for was that it backs up everything each night—including messages in draft mode? We have over two years' worth of communication. It's a strong case against both of you."

Barney let out a slow sigh. "I'm doomed."

"In this world, yes," Emma said, "but there is still hope for you spiritually."

Barney shook his head. "No, there isn't."

"There's always hope."

"Not for me." He leaned forward and rested his head on the table, cradling it in his arms.

Emma sensed there was no point in arguing with him any further. "One thing I am curious about is why the password to your secret email account is 'Emma'."

Barney sat up but didn't gloat. "I appreciate your curiosity and will explain all on your next visit. But you must bring Montgomery with you. I insist."

"The prison doesn't allow animals to visit," Emma said.

"Surely they'll make an exception for you as High Priestess."

"The rules that apply to everyone apply to me too."

Barney stood. He glared down at Emma. "No Montgomery means no answers."

3

CHLOE'S NEWS

After eating breakfast with the priests the next morning, Emma and Montgomery walked over to Chloe and Gabe's table. Emma's best friend and the girl's grandfather stood as Emma approached. The trio headed to Ashley's salon to drop off Montgomery for the day.

"I have exciting news," Chloe said to Emma. "Over the weekend we looked at bigger houses, and Dad put in an offer. Last night they accepted. It has four bedrooms and three baths. We'll each have our own room, with one to spare. It's vacant, and we can move in right away."

"So exciting!" Emma said. "You, Gabe, and your dad can spend more time together. That will be good. The only downside is I'm losing a roommate."

"Thanks for letting me stay with you," Chloe said. "But it's better for our friendship if I move out. I'm not the easiest person to room with."

"But we made it work," Emma said. "That's what matters."

"It's going to be great, the three of us living together as a family," Chloe said. "If only Mom was still alive. Then it would be perfect."

"Chloe," Gabe said softly. "Your mother *is* alive."

Chloe shook her head. "Dad said she died when I was little."

"To be correct, she left when you were little. Though she may have seemed dead to your father, and it was perhaps in your best interest for him to communicate that she had passed, the reality is that she is very much alive. I met her in a homeless shelter a few years ago. We reconciled with each other, and we've been in contact ever since."

Chloe stopped walking and stomped her foot. "Then why hasn't she come home?"

Gabe looked intently into his granddaughter's eyes and laid a gentle hand on her shoulder.

"Because she's embarrassed about the mistakes she's made. She's ashamed and carries much guilt. Your mother fears that coming home after all these years will cause you more pain than she's already inflicted upon you."

Chloe stomped her foot again. Twice. A tear formed in her right eye and leaked out. Many more followed it. "We'd have forgiven her. We'd have offered her grace. Dad has been great in raising me, but a girl needs a mom too!"

"Though you may indeed be at a point in your young life to forgive your mother and offer her grace, I'm not sure your father will be that magnanimous—at least not at this point."

Chloe wiped the tears from her cheeks. "But shouldn't he be the one to make that decision?"

Gabe took in a slow breath. "You present an astute query into the situation, but I sense your father is not as prepared to offer her grace as you are. It will require patience on our part and concerted prayer before we consider broaching the subject with him."

Having reached Ashley's salon, Emma walked Montgomery inside, leaving her best friend and her mentor to continue their conversation.

Ashley looked up from a laptop as Emma unclipped Montgomery's leash. He dashed to his water bowl and lapped twice. Then he scooted to his bed and snuggled down, his eyes gazing up at the two women.

"Are you computerizing your schedule?" Emma tipped her head toward the laptop.

Ashley looked up and laughed. "Paper works just fine for me." She pointed at her spiral-bound schedule book. "Lane set up the laptop for me to help the communications department. I can process email and text messages in between hair appointments. That way I can be productive all day long while staying here at the salon. It's working out great and makes the day fly by."

Emma groaned. "Will we ever get caught up on the communications backlog?"

"We're just about there. Your fellow students—your disciples, as Mr. Gabe calls them—are being released into the areas where they want to work. The students from the Priest Academy will finish getting us caught up. Then we'll see if Beatrice and Kayla, along with my help, can stay on top of things."

Emma scrutinized Ashley's left hand and narrowed her eyes. "What's on your finger?"

Ashley grinned. "It's a ring tattoo." She extended her hand for Emma to see. "You said the Holy Text never mentions wedding rings, but people today expect them. So Topher and I decided we'd solve that by getting tattoos. They're supposed to last forever, just like our marriage."

"Great idea!" Emma said. She cocked her head to the side. "Did it hurt much?"

"Did it ever! But Topher had a worse go of it. I guess I'm tougher than he is."

Emma blessed Ashley for her work and said goodbye to Montgomery as she left the salon.

Gabe and Chloe awaited her outside. Her friend was glowing. "Grandpa says Mom lives in a halfway house about thirty minutes away. He's going to see if we can visit. I'm so excited!"

Emma reached for her friend's hand and extended her other arm toward Gabe. "Sovereign, bless their meeting. Restore Chloe's mom into the family. Amen."

The trio opened their eyes and walked toward the school building. Gabe fell behind them as he fumbled with his phone.

Emma broke the silence on their thoughtful walk. "Ashley says you're about caught up with communications and everyone's moving into where they want to work."

"Yep! Christopher has been reassigning us this week," Chloe said. "Lane has his tech office about set up, Natalie is helping at the clinic, and Grace is learning how to give Temple tours. Joshua has been working with Gavin at the old sanctuary, and Lauren has been working with Ezra at the ancient Temple. Oh, and Kayla's helping Beatrice with communication."

Emma took all this in. "What about you?"

"I've got your social media pages all set up and am fine-tuning phase one of your website. Lane will help me go live tomorrow."

Emma would've known this had she remembered to hold their Wednesday morning meeting yesterday. But she pushed aside the impulse to scold herself and instead celebrated the progress. "Great news! I'm so excited for everyone."

"But there's one thing we need to talk about," Chloe said. "Please keep an open mind."

Emma grew curious. "What?"

"A lot of people have asked for an autographed photo of you."

Emma shook her head. "I don't want to

promote myself. We must point people to the Sovereign.

"I knew you wouldn't like it," Chloe said. "But I think you'll like this." She handed Emma a partial sheet of paper. "Here's a mockup."

Emma studied it.

"It's a bookmark," Chloe said, "for when people read Scripture."

It featured a picture of the Holy Text, with key supporting verses under it. Emma flipped the bookmark over. There in the middle was a picture of her—the very thing she opposed. But her signature partially covered the upper left of her face and a Scripture reference was over the lower right: Wisdom 27.42. The passage was below it.

Above her picture, in large letters, was a quote. Emma read it aloud: "Read and study the Holy Text every day. It's made a difference in my life, and I pray it will in yours too." Emma paused. "Though I agree with this, I didn't say it."

"But you just did!" Chloe grinned.

Emma tossed back her head with a snicker. "I approve this bookmark. But no 8 x 10 glossy pictures of me."

"I'm still figuring that one out," Chloe said.

Emma was ready to tell her not to bother, but

her vibrating phone distracted her. It was a text from Topher. "He wants to schedule my driving practice this afternoon," Emma told Chloe.

"The rest of us finished our driving practice Monday afternoon when you were in the capital," Chloe said. "Since last Saturday didn't work, and this Saturday is out too, Christopher and Topher pushed hard to finish on Monday. You're the only one left."

Emma reviewed her afternoon schedule aloud. "I'm meeting with some priests at 1:00 to discuss having daily chapel services. At 2:00 is our regular meeting with all the priests to talk about the Holy Text. But I'm open after 3:00." She texted Topher. He agreed.

As the girls reached the entrance to the school building, Gabe caught up with them. "I have received some most delightful news, Chloe. I engaged in a text message conversation with your mother and informed her of your yearning to connect with her, along with your intention to offer her forgiveness and grace. She is available to meet with us this afternoon. Would you like me to confirm this with her?"

Chloe's face said yes, but she looked at Emma.

"If I go, it will delay your website another day. Is that okay?"

Emma bobbed her head. "Meeting your mom is more important."

Gabe smiled. "I suggest we plan our departure for immediately after the conclusion of our noon-time nourishment. I will inform your mother of our expected arrival at 1:30 p.m."

4

EMMA'S GAFFES

When Emma entered the classroom, she didn't go to her regular seat. Instead, she walked up to Jennifer, who sat at the front of the room at her desk.

"I forgot all about our Wednesday morning update about everyone becoming a priest," Emma said. "Can we do it today?"

"Certainly," Jennifer said. "I had it on my schedule for yesterday and wanted to give you the opportunity to take the lead. When you didn't, I assumed you had nothing to share."

"That's my fault," Emma said. "Being at the capital on Monday has thrown me off a bit."

Jennifer nodded her agreement. "By the way, thanks for suggesting your father and mother mentor David and me. We'll meet twice a week until our wedding, which will be in two months."

"Or you could do it next Saturday."

Jennifer shook her head. "The dates are filling up fast, and the next available one isn't for two months. Besides, David and I want to buy a house before we get married. Neither of our apartments is big enough for two."

"Check with Chloe's dad," Emma said. "He just bought a bigger house and needs to sell his old one. I think they call it a starter home: two bedrooms and one bath."

"That would be perfect," Jennifer said.

Chloe edged up and scribbled something on a scrap of paper. "Here's Dad's number. He was planning on listing it next week after we move, but maybe you can save him the trouble."

"Thank you," Jennifer said to Chloe. The teacher turned her attention back to Emma. "I see that everyone's here. You may begin."

Emma spun around. "Sorry, I forgot to do this yesterday. So this is the Thursday edition of our Wednesday meeting." She gave them a relaxed smile. "Chloe told me you're each moving into the area you want to focus on. That's great! But having a mentor is also important. If you're still looking for one, text me and I'll help get you connected. Also, let me know if there's anything else you want to talk about."

Emma moved to her seat in the classroom, and everyone began their studies.

With diligent focus, she and Joshua both finished their classwork forty-five minutes early and went for a walk before lunch.

"Sorry for not spending much time with you lately," Emma said. "That's on me."

Joshua reached for her hand. "No worries. I've been kind of busy too. Why don't you come over to my house for dinner tonight? I'm sure Mom will be fine with it."

"Rain check? I hope to visit Barney in prison tonight."

"Okay then, dinner on Friday. Tonight I'll go with you on your visit."

Emma wanted to tell him she was perfectly fine to go on her own, but she didn't. She knew he wanted to protect her. Instead of feeling smothered by his offer, she felt cherished. "That would be perfect."

Without a word, he squeezed her hand twice.

Emma's heart fluttered, and she tipped her head onto his shoulder. "You're amazing."

"I think the same thing about you."

"Gabe will drive," Emma said. "We'll leave at five and eat when we get back."

As they neared the cafeteria for lunch, Fred awaited her, with feet firmly planted and arms crossed. Emma let go of Joshua's hand. She sighed. *What did I do wrong now?* She wouldn't have to wait long to find out.

"What's this I hear about you starting a chapel service?" Fred asked. "You should've cleared it with Christopher, Mark, and me first."

Emma blinked back her frustration. "I thought I should see if the priests were interested before I bothered you guys with it. You're all so busy."

"I appreciate your concern for our schedules," Fred said. "What I don't appreciate is a priest asking me about something I knew nothing about. It was disconcerting, frustrating, and embarrassing."

Emma sighed once more. "I messed up . . . again. Sorry. But I thought I was doing things in the right order this time."

Now it was Fred's turn to sigh. "I too often forget that you're fifteen. You still have a lot to learn. In general, keep me informed of any ideas you have that affect staff, operations, or ministry.

Then I can loop in Christopher, Mark, or Topher as appropriate."

"Got it!" Emma said. "That helps a lot."

"Are we good going forward?" Fred asked.

"I think so, but I scheduled a meeting with some priests at 1:00 to discuss this. Should I cancel?"

"Since it's just a discussion, you may proceed. I'll apprise Mark."

"I also have another question for you," Emma said. "I feel a prompting from the Divine Spirit, but it's kind of hard to explain."

"Do your best," Fred said.

"Chloe just found out her mother is still alive. Gabe is taking her this afternoon so they can meet. I've been praying for their family's restoration. There are two things we can do to help. One is to move Chloe's mom closer, and the other is to help her grow spiritually. We can do both if we let her move into a room in the palace."

"Interesting." Fred brought his hand to his beard and stroked it. "Had anyone else made such a request, I'd have immediately dismissed it. Yet coming from you—given your record of astute supernatural insight—I'll give it serious consideration. Let me discuss this with Gabe. I'll offer it as an option should he deem it to be the right step to take."

With a slow exhale, Emma released the tension that had been building inside her, a smile sprouting on her face. "Thank you."

Fred nodded. "I commend you for bringing this to my attention so we can handle it properly and you not barreling ahead on your own. Well done!"

5

EMMA'S PROGRESS

Once Emma's team had joined her in the cafeteria for their working lunch, Fred began. "To make sure we're on the same page, here are some updates. First, Ezra has been conducting daily services at the Temple this week. We've not announced it, so attendance is sparse. But we're ready to promote it. Next week, Elizabeth Butler will begin teaching an online class about the Holy Text. She'll also start an in-person class for homeschoolers. Last, Emma will work with some priests to discuss holding daily chapel services in the old sanctuary. She'll keep us apprised of developments."

"About the old sanctuary," Emma said. "Ever since we reopened it, we've all called it the old sanctuary. It's convenient, but it doesn't sound the best. How about we call it the Jacob G. Turrum Auditorium in honor of the last high priest? Turrum Auditorium for short?"

"That's a brilliant idea," Gavin said. "Some people who attend our services there want a more appropriate name. They object to the word *old*. Calling it Turrum Auditorium is much more respectful."

Emma scanned her team. "Shall we do it?" Everyone nodded. Fred confirmed their decision.

"And I'd like to propose," Mark added, "that we rename the new sanctuary the Emma Barlow Auditorium."

Emma shook her head vigorously. "Certainly not. That's an honor I don't deserve or want." She paused. "It's so bright and airy. Why don't we call it the Sunshine Auditorium because the Sovereign is the source of true light?"

Everyone murmured their assent, and Fred verified their conclusion. "Sunshine Auditorium it is. Any other business?"

Emma partially raised her hand. "My friends are moving into the areas where they want to work at the Temple, but three of them still need a mentor."

"Text me their names," Mark said, "and I'll get with the priests to make it happen."

"One more item," Fred added, "is that we need to ease Gabe and Joshua into some low-key participation in the Sunday services. When I move to the capital, we need to have some support for Mark and Emma so they're not carrying the entire weight of the Sunday services on their own. We'll also be giving Gavin the opportunity to speak at the old sanctuary . . . I mean, the Turrum Auditorium."

A couple of hours later, Emma slid into the car and started it. She turned to Topher sitting next to her. "Where to, boss?"

"Make two laps around the entire facility and then park in front of the admin building. Choose a spot next to another car. Back in."

"No problem."

"You seem quite confident today. Why the huge change?"

"A big reason is prayer. But it didn't hurt driving my golf cart around here on Sunday." Emma chuckled. "Plus, I won't have Joshua and Chloe kibitzing in the backseat."

"Do you need quiet to concentrate as you drive?"

Emma eased the car forward. "Talking is fine. It's their snickers and whispers that got to me."

"I was going to tell them to stop, but you were bantering with them."

"I was trying to act like it wasn't bothering me, but it was. A lot. That's why I kept making mistakes with my driving." Emma reached the end of the road and turned left.

"Remember to signal your turns," Topher said.

"Even in a parking lot when there's no one around?"

"It's good practice for when you drive on the streets."

When Emma neared the next turn, she flicked on her left turn signal, slowed the car, and made a perfect turn.

"Well done."

Emma made two laps and then parked the car as instructed.

"Excellent," Topher said. "But can you do it without a backup camera?"

"Doubtful. But it doesn't matter since I have one."

"Older cars don't. Or it could stop working.

Make a lap in the opposite direction and park back here, this time without using the camera."

Emma did.

"Great job. Now drive to the old . . . to the Turrum Auditorium. Look for a spot to parallel park."

"With or without using the backup cam?"

Topher chuckled. "First with and then without."

Emma did and then drove to Topher's next destination.

"How did your meeting about starting a chapel service go?" Topher asked.

"We quickly agreed on the format," Emma said. "An opening song, a Scripture passage, and a short but meaningful teaching. We'll end with a blessing. We're aiming for about ten minutes, fifteen max."

"Sounds great. What time?"

"That's where it gets messy," Emma said. "I was thinking mid-morning. Mark suggested before work. Ezra said afternoon so it wouldn't conflict with daily services in the Temple. And another priest thought evening was the best option."

"That's a conundrum."

Emma glanced at Topher. "Does conundrum mean a difficult problem?"

"Yes, indeed."

"Though we could end up doing all four times, we want to start with one," Emma said. "We'll survey the staff to find out what time will work best to begin with."

For the next hour and a half, Emma followed all of Topher's instructions. She had only one bobble. He had said to circle to the left, and she went right. But everything else earned his praise.

At five o'clock she pulled up to the Sunshine Auditorium where Joshua and Chloe waited for her. "You did an excellent job today," Topher said. "I proclaim you ready to get your provisional license."

Emma turned off the car and got out. With much fanfare, Joshua and Chloe yelped, jumped, and clapped. She responded with a grin and a curtsy.

6

HUGS

Emma walked up to Joshua and hugged him. She glanced at Chloe. The girl's eyes were red. "Did meeting your mom not go well?"

"She won't tell me." Joshua crossed his arms and scowled.

Emma glared at him. Turning back to Chloe, she softened her gaze. "Tell me about it."

Chloe shrugged. "I'm glad I met her, and we'll see her again Saturday afternoon, but it didn't go at all like I expected. Not. At. All."

"What did you expect?"

"I expected she'd be excited. She wasn't. I expected she'd give me a hug. She didn't. I expected she'd come back with us. But she said she wasn't ready." Chloe's upper lip quivered.

Emma wrapped her arms around her friend and squeezed tight. "It's going to take time. We need to be patient. Remember that your grandpa said it would take concerted prayer."

"Yeah, whatever that means." Chloe sniffled.

"It means to pray a lot," Emma whispered to Chloe.

"Grandpa and I prayed most of the way back. He kept his eyes open, of course."

"I've been praying too," Emma said.

Joshua clenched his jaw. "So have I."

Chloe stiffened.

Emma narrowed her eyes at Joshua. She knew he was just trying to help, but he wasn't helping at all.

He shrugged and walked away.

Emma released her grasp of Chloe, who wiped at her eyes. "Will you go with us on Saturday?"

"I can leave after Christopher and Angie's wedding. But why do you want me to go? I don't know your mom or anything about her."

"I feel brave when you're around. And peace seems to go where you go. We definitely need peace.

And someone to keep the conversation going so there isn't so much awkward silence."

"Count me in."

"Thanks!" Chloe's eyes fluttered as she turned to leave.

As Chloe walked away, Joshua edged up to Emma, and the pair waved goodbye.

"Sorry," Joshua said. "I was just trying to help."

"I know you were, but sometimes the best thing a guy can say to a crying girl is nothing."

"When my mom cries, it means she wants to talk. Same with you."

"We're special. What about Sarah?"

"When my sister cries, it means she wants a hug."

"And no talking, right?"

"Correct. Talking only makes her cry more."

"Have I made my point?"

"Got it!"

Emma gave Joshua a hug. It lasted until Gabe drove up.

As the purr of the engine grew closer, Joshua dropped his embrace and turned toward the vehicle. "Cool car!" He strode to it.

Gabe smiled. "It belongs to my granddaughter."

Joshua scowled. "Chloe doesn't even have her license. Why does she have a car?"

"My son had allocated funds to buy her a used automobile when she turned sixteen and obtained authorization to drive a motorized vehicle. When I relocated to his abode, I required transportation to arrive here each morning in a timely fashion and return each evening. To smartly address this situation, he purchased said vehicle ahead of schedule for me to drive on a short-term basis until my granddaughter is permitted to use it legally."

Emma walked up to the car and slid her arm around Joshua's waist. "So Chloe's dad bought this car for her, and you're driving it until she turns sixteen."

Gabe scowled at her. "That's what I just said."

Emma and Joshua shared a quick glance and Emma giggled.

Gabe snorted. "Shall we depart?"

It was the shortest, most concise thing Gabe had ever said.

7

NO HUGS

Emma walked up to the counter at the prison. Joshua and Gabe flanked her, one on each side. There sat the same woman Emma had seen last night.

"Who are you here to see?" the woman asked, again without a glance.

"Barney Clark, please," Emma said.

The woman looked up with a start and gave Emma a smile. "Welcome back . . . Emma. But he can have only one visitor at a time. You'll need to take turns. Do you want to go first?"

"Please," Emma said.

The woman typed on her computer and clicked the mouse twice. "Please sign in." She pointed to the visitor sheet. "Then have a seat." She tipped her head toward the waiting area. "It shouldn't be long."

As Joshua and Gabe moved toward the chairs, Emma unshouldered her backpack. "I have something for Barney. It's his copy of the Holy Text. Will you give it to him?"

"I'm sorry, but visitors aren't allowed to give gifts to prisoners. It's prohibited."

Emma had half expected that response, but she had to try. "I understand."

But then the woman leaned forward and whispered, "Given who you are and that it's the Holy Text, I'll make sure he gets it. But don't tell anyone."

Emma extended the book but then paused. "I don't want you to get in trouble or anything."

"Don't worry. The worst they could do is fire me." The corners of the woman's lips twitched up. "And that might be a blessing in disguise."

"If you're ever looking for a new job, check the help-wanted page on the Temple website," Emma said. "Drop my name if you apply."

"I may just do that." The woman took the Holy Text from Emma and slid it into a drawer behind the counter. "I'll see that he gets it."

Emma thanked the woman and headed toward

Joshua and Gabe, but the woman stopped her. "He's ready for you, and you may proceed."

Emma moved toward the double doors, and they opened as she approached. She walked through and was soon facing a grinning Barney, who sat at the same table as he had the night before.

But his smirk faded. "Where's Montgomery? I said you had to bring him, or I wouldn't talk to you."

"Animals are prohibited."

"Then you must leave."

"Do you really want to kick out the only person who wants to see you?"

Barney let out a slow sigh. "Very well." He gestured to the chair facing him. "Have a seat."

Emma sat. Though she really wanted to know why his email password was 'Emma,' she resolved to say nothing and let him talk first.

At last he did. "Did you know I was married?"

"No way!" Emma said. "Then why did you prohibit the priests from getting married and the staff from dating?"

"I consider it a perk of leadership."

"I consider it a double standard."

Barney snorted. "Tomayto, tomahto.

Regardless, we were married for over ten years. Her name was Em."

"Short for Emma?"

"That's a good guess, but no. It was short for Emily. We pledged our lives and our marriage to serve the Sovereign. I became His Royal Eminence, and Em was my Senior Aide. After years of waiting, we were at last going to have a child. It was a girl. We picked the name Emma." Barney closed his eyes and inhaled with deliberation. He clenched his jaw.

Emma reached out and laid her hand on his. "What happened?"

Barney opened his eyes. They were sad. "A drunk driver . . . in the middle of the afternoon. He T-boned our car. I was fine, but my beloved Em suffered severe injuries."

"What about the baby?"

"The accident jolted Em into labor. An ambulance rushed us to the hospital. I pleaded with the Sovereign to spare their lives. But no! Our so-called loving Lord completely ignored me. They both died. We deserved better. We earned it. In complete despair, I renounced the Sovereign and gave my life to the evil one. That was sixteen years ago."

Emma gasped. "So your daughter would have been my age."

"Precisely."

"Does seeing me remind you of her?"

"Every day." Barney moaned. "Sometimes I look at you and feel only pain—even loathing. Other times I want to embrace you in love, like the daughter the Sovereign killed."

"The Sovereign didn't kill your baby," Emma said gently. "A drunk driver did."

"Yeah, whatever. First, a drunk driver took my wife and baby. Then you took my work and my freedom."

Emma strove to maintain her gentle tone. "Don't blame me for your mistakes."

"It was wrong for the Sovereign to ignore my prayers," Barney countered.

"The Sovereign heard your prayers. It's just that you didn't get the answers you wanted."

"The Sovereign could have stopped that man from driving."

"That would have taken away his free will," Emma said. "The Sovereign lets everyone make their own decisions and seldom interferes with how they live their lives—even if it's wrong."

"Well then, the Sovereign should have kept my wife and daughter alive and healed them both."

"Miracles sometimes occur, like when the Sovereign raised Joshua from the dead. But if miracles happened every time we wanted them, they'd just be normal events. We wouldn't need miracles anymore."

"That's all fine and good," Barney sputtered, "but I still hold the Sovereign accountable for killing my family."

"I pray you'll one day have a different perspective," Emma said, "that you'll repent and the Sovereign will restore you into a right relationship."

"You could help move your little prayer forward with action."

Emma cocked her head to the side. "Like what?"

"My legal team tells me that aside from receiving a pardon, I'll spend the rest of my life in prison."

"The Prime Minister can't pardon you, remember?"

"The Prime Minister isn't the only one who can offer pardons. So can the High Priest. You can pardon me."

Emma shook her head. "You broke the law and deserve punishment."

"Emma, I beg you. I'm a changed man."

Emma looked at his visage in the spiritual realm. His appearance bore the same glossy black as always. "No. You are not a changed man."

Barney leaned forward, grabbed Emma's wrists, and shook her. "Grant me a pardon!"

"Barney, you're hurting me."

"Pardon me!"

"In the name of the Sovereign, I command you to let me go. Now!"

Barney's grip on Emma released as his chair jerked back with a metallic screech, carrying him away as it scraped along the tile floor. After traveling five feet, both toppled to the side. He landed on the floor with a thump.

A guard ran up and tased Barney. When a second guard arrived, they grabbed him by his arms and dragged him away.

8

ORGAN MUSIC

As Emma walked to breakfast, she continued thinking about what Barney had said and done the night before. Though she had pleaded with the official in charge to not punish Barney for assaulting her, she doubted he would offer Barney mercy.

Emma finished eating before most of the priests. She stood and extended her arms out at her sides. "May the Sovereign bless you in your work today. Amen."

She lowered her arms, but she had more on her mind. "Also, will you pray for me? A couple Sundays ago I said I would sing a portion of the service, just like we read about in the Holy Text. Scripture gives us the words, but I'm struggling with the tune. Please pray that I'll have supernatural insight."

The priests agreed, and Mark stood to pray for her right then. His words still reverberated in her mind as she dropped Montgomery off at Ashley's salon. She listened to the Sovereign for insight. Soon divine words formed in her mind, but they weren't the words she sought.

Work ahead on your school assignments.

Emma had no idea what that had to do with finding the right tune for Sunday's service, but she would obey her Lord's command.

Working diligently on the day's schoolwork, Emma finished faster than usual. Then she dove into Monday's assignments. Though she was usually the first to leave school each morning, today her classmates left as she continued to work. First, Chloe and Lane left. When Joshua finished, he gave her a questioning look. She shook her head. He nodded and left too. As noon approached, half of Emma's classmates had finished for the day, while she continued working.

By the time she left for lunch, she had half of Monday's assignments completed. As she approached the cafeteria, she jogged—the best she could—to catch up with Fred on the path before her.

He turned to look her way as she huffed up. "I heard from the Prison Oversight Authority," he said. "They want to move ahead with Michael's proposal. He and I are flying there to finalize details on Monday."

"Can I tag along?" Emma asked.

"Toward what end?"

"Since they wanted my input about the proposal, it might help if I'm there at this meeting too."

"Did the Sovereign tell you to be there?"

"Maybe. At least indirectly. But I also felt a prompting to visit the Prime Minister and try to see her. She needs to repent, and I doubt anyone else will be brave enough to tell her."

"I'll get you a ticket," Fred said. "We'll leave mid-afternoon on Sunday, just like last week. You and Michael can fly back Monday night. I'll stay an extra day to investigate places for us to hold our Sunday services."

After lunch, Emma joined the Priest Academy for the afternoon, at least for most of it. Though she had intended to observe, Mrs. Butler asked her to start the class with prayer and to share any thoughts she might have. Emma did and then retreated to the back of the room so she could watch and not be a distraction. What she saw pleased her. The students meshed well and were eager to learn about the Holy Text.

Just before 2:00, Emma slipped out to meet with the priests to discuss the Holy Text. To her surprise, all the Priest Academy students followed her.

Emma addressed the expanded group and led them in a lively discussion about Wisdom chapter 97. An hour later, she was back with the Priest Academy students in their regular classroom. She stayed with them until it was time for Joshua's mother to pick them up for dinner.

Arriving at Joshua's house, a surprise awaited Emma. Her family was there: her mom and dad and both sibs. As Emma and Joshua set the table, the dads talked about soccer, and the moms discussed a new cooking show. Organ music played in the background.

Joshua's sister, Sarah, bounded up to him. "Can I show Hailey and Brayden your treehouse?"

Joshua crossed his arms and scowled at her, but then he relaxed and smiled. "I think it's time for me to pass the treehouse on to you. It's yours now. Have fun!" Giggling, the three middle schoolers dashed out the back door and scampered up the ladder to reach the grand structure. Montgomery darted after them and waited at the base of the tree, as if standing guard.

After a few more minute, the moms put the food in serving bowls, as the dads whisked each dish to the table. Emma poured the drinks, while Joshua went outside to retrieve Sarah, Hailey, and Brayden.

With the intermingling aromas of the meal teasing their appetites, the nine of them selected seats around the table. Brayden pushed his sister out of the way so he could sit next to Sarah. Hailey shook her head and sat on his other side. Once seated, everyone held hands.

Joshua gave the meal's opening prayer. "Lord, thank you for this food. Bless our time together. May we bring glory to you. Amen."

A flutter of activity immediately followed the amen as they passed the food and piled their plates with savory roast beef, tasty noodles, fresh green beans, and piping hot oatmeal rolls. Emma licked her lips in anticipation as she buttered her roll.

Joshua had just popped some meat into his mouth when Emma's dad asked him about his work at the Temple. Joshua held up his index finger to signal that he couldn't talk. He chewed quickly and swallowed with a gulp. "I'm working with Gavin at the Turrum Auditorium . . . that's what we're now calling the old sanctuary. I'm going to start helping with the Sunday service. I'm so excited . . . and a bit nervous too."

"I'm sure you'll do fine," Emma's dad said.

"I sure hope so," Joshua said. "This Sunday I'll read the passage from the Holy Text before Frederick gives the message."

"Mark will speak for both services at the Sunshine Auditorium," Emma said. "That's what we're now calling the new auditorium. Including the two ancient services at the Temple, I'll help in all five services, but it will all be minor parts."

"A break—of sorts—is probably a good idea for you," Emma's mom said. "You've been pushing yourself hard ever since you became High Priestess."

"Frederick will soon move to the capital," Emma said. "So that everything for the Sunday services doesn't fall just to Mark and me, we'll be getting Joshua involved, along with Gabe and Gavin."

Their discussion moved on to other things as they balanced eating with talking. When everyone finished, Emma's mom wiped her lips with her napkin and laid it on her plate. "This was a wonderful meal and a great time together. Let's do it again. Soon. We'll host."

Everyone agreed this was a great idea. They settled on a date.

Sarah rose to get her copy of the Holy Text. She read History 163. Everyone listened intently.

When she closed the book, Emma's mom spoke. "That was very nice, Sarah. Reading the Holy Text after a meal is a practice we've recently started."

Frustrated, Emma glared at her mom.

"We've been doing it for as long as I can remember," Sarah said.

"I wish I could say the same thing," Emma's mom said. "When Emma suggested it, we told her no and refused to discuss it. But we eventually realized she was right."

Emma relaxed her scowl. Her mother had listened to her after all, even though it had taken a while to react.

With dinner over and the Holy Text read, Sarah gave the meal's concluding prayer. "Lord, thank you for our food and our time together. Please be with us for the rest of the evening. Amen."

"Amen," everyone else said. They stood and

helped clean up. The connection between the two families thrilled Emma. As the last of the dishes were done, Joshua's dad posed a question. "Shall we retreat to the den and have a sing-along?"

Emma froze.

Her family listened to music but didn't sing. And they definitely weren't into organs.

9

BARNEY'S BATTLE

Emma pulled back the covers and slid into her bed — the bed in her room at her parents' house. It felt so good, yet something was off. Though it had only been a few months since she had left, this was no longer her home. She lived at the Temple. That was her home now. That's where she belonged.

Montgomery jumped on the bed and snuggled next to her. Her mom would freak out if she knew a dog was on the bed. So Mom would never need to find out. Never, ever.

As Emma reviewed her day, she had much to celebrate. Dinner at Joshua's had gone great. His family and hers fit well together. Though she had feared the organ sing-along would put a damper on the evening, her parents gave it a try and enjoyed it. The sibs even joined in, though she figured Brayden did it just to impress Sarah. Afterward he had said, "It wasn't as lame as I thought it would be."

They stayed too late, and Emma's mom invited her to come home with them. It was only two minutes away, while the trip across town to the Temple would take half an hour. Emma agreed. It was her first time back at their house since she had moved into the High Priest's residence on the Temple grounds.

Emma wanted to close her eyes and go to sleep. She was certainly ready to nod off. But she remembered she hadn't yet read the Holy Text. She grabbed her phone and pulled up the app. It would have to do.

You can skip tonight, came the Sovereign's words implanted in Emma's mind. *You have my blessing.*

No! If I skip one night, it'll be too easy to skip two. Plus, I want to keep my streak going.

She brought up Wisdom 98 and began reading. About halfway through the passage, her eyelids strained to close. *Just for a second,* she promised herself, allowing her lids to flutter shut.

A commotion roused her from her slumber. Booming noises and flashing lights bombarded her being. Terrified, her eyes popped open, but everything was still and dark. The only sound was Montgomery's peaceful breathing. Emma peered into the spiritual realm. Chaos swirled about her, but she didn't panic. She knew just what to do. *In the name of the Sovereign, I declare this room, this house, and this property to be a safe place, free of all evil spirits and demonic influences.*

The command had barely formed in her mind when the dark demons fled her spirit's presence with terrifying shrieks of horror. As they retreated, light filled the spiritual space around Emma. Though some of it emitted from herself, most beamed down from heaven. Four angels positioned themselves, one in each corner of the room. As if standing guard, they held a shimmering sword in one hand and the Holy Text in the other. They quoted Scripture in unison. The demons gasped in horror and retreated even further.

Basking in the Sovereign's approval, peace filled Emma. She closed her eyes to return to her slumber, but the Sovereign's instruction stopped her. *Contact Barney in the spiritual realm.*

Why? Emma asked.

Just do it.

Emma stilled her breathing and focused her thoughts. Within seconds, her spirit eased away from her body and sped at a dazzling pace toward the prison.

She found Barney easily enough. As his body tossed in the bed, his detached spirit trembled nearby, cowering in the corner of his cell. It was as jet-black as always.

Emma slowed her approach. "Barney," she whispered in the spiritual realm. "Barney. It's Emma. Can we talk?"

The black blob rotated toward her. It attempted to elongate itself, as if trying to stand, but it failed. "Oh, my Emma." Barney's spirit groaned. "My dear, dear Emma. I am so sorry I attacked you. I promise never to hurt you again. Please forgive me."

"No worries. It's all good."

"To what do I owe your unexpected appearance?"

"The Sovereign told me to visit you."

"How I wish I could hear from the Sovereign like you do," Barney said supernaturally. "Will you give me that ability?"

"Since you rejected the Sovereign and turned

your soul over to the devil, you cannot receive what the Sovereign wants to give you. You must first renounce evil and remove the stronghold it has on you. That will make room for the Sovereign."

"I can't do that," Barney protested.

"You barred the Sovereign from your life and embraced the devil. Only you can reverse that."

"You're nothing but a worthless little girl!" Barney's spirit screamed. "Away with you. Away from my presence. Never return."

Emma recoiled at his sudden change. The white light from her core dimmed a bit, but only for a moment. Then it rebounded even brighter. She summoned supernatural courage from the Sovereign. Her white glow expanded to fill the room.

"Be gone!" Barney shrieked. "I never want to see you again!"

Emma strove to remain calm. "I don't think you mean that."

"I do," Barney insisted. "No!" he screamed. "I don't."

"Are you arguing with yourself?" Emma asked.

"I don't know. Maybe." Barney's black blob shuddered. It tittered. Like a tire going flat, it shrunk to the size of a tennis ball, resting on the corner of his bed. "Help me, Emma. Please."

Emma moved her spirit closer to his.

"Stop tormenting me, Emma!"

"Your battle isn't with me. It's within you."

"Oh, what a wretched man I am. I don't do what I want to do and do what I don't want. It is a profound misery that I can no longer abide."

Emma's spirit surrounded his. "Tell the devil to leave your being and never come back."

"I want to," Barney said, "but I can't. I'm afraid." His spirit shuddered once again, shrinking still smaller until it was the size of a ping-pong ball.

"Repeat after me," Emma said. "Devil, I kick you out of my life. Leave me alone and never come back."

Barney repeated her words but at a mere whisper. His glossy, jet-black spirit shook and began to sob, slowly at first and then uncontrollably. In seconds, it morphed into a flat black.

"Emma, I'm empty. So empty. I'm alone. So alone."

"Repent of your sins and give your life over to the Sovereign."

"I'm too ashamed," Barney sputtered. "I

rejected the Sovereign and don't deserve mercy. I deserve judgment. I deserve punishment."

"The Sovereign's mercy means not getting the judgment and punishment you deserve. Instead, by grace, you will receive good things you don't deserve."

"I can't repent of my sins," Barney said. "At least not yet. I'm not ready."

"Saying not now," Emma said, "is the same as saying no. Don't tell the Sovereign no. Say yes. Just believe."

Barney's spirit remained quiet. His spirit shrank to the size of a pea and trembled as it slid back into his body with a thump.

10

FAMILY MATTERS

Emma stirred at the sound of her bedroom door creaking open.

"Emma," her mom whispered. "Emma, you need to get up. You've slept in long enough."

Emma turned toward the voice and forced her eyes open. As she did, Montgomery stirred too.

"Emma!" her mother hissed. "Get that dog off my bed. Now!"

Her mother's stern reprimand showed a restrained calm for the moment, but it wouldn't stay that way.

Emma had to act fast before her mother went ballistic. She jumped out of bed and scooped up Montgomery, bewildered at all the commotion.

Cradling him in her arms, Emma ruffled the top of his head and gave him a quick kiss. "Who's a good boy? You are. You're such a good boy." She lowered him to the ground, and he jumped out of her hands as he neared the floor. He turned and looked up at the bed.

"Don't you dare," Emma's mother warned through gritted teeth. She brought her hands to her hips and cocked her head to glare at Emma. She let out a slow sigh. "I'm going to pretend I never saw this. And I don't want to ever see it again." She turned and stomped out of the room.

Emma took the puppy with her into the bathroom. "Stay here, and don't irritate Mom anymore." Emma turned on the water and slid into the shower. The hot water felt so good. It awoke her body, preparing her for the day.

When she had first moved to live in the High Priest's residence, she had only taken some of her clothes with her, intending to get the rest later. Later never happened. As a result, she had a nice selection to choose from today. She got dressed and began packing her remaining clothes. She finished just as Hailey walked in to call her for breakfast.

Her dad gave the opening blessing, and they began eating. After Emma poured syrup on her waffle, she looked up to scrutinize the sibs. She had last sat at this table only two months ago, but they looked bigger now. Older. Certainly more mature. They were growing up, and she was missing it.

Though she was glad to be High Priestess and relished all that she did—well, most of it—the position came at a cost. One huge sacrifice was less time to spend with her family.

After offering Emma a second waffle, her mom paused, looking at her intently. "I'm sorry for dismissing you when you asked that we read the Holy Text after dinner."

"No worries," Emma said. "The main thing is that you're doing it now."

"We read after *every* meal," her mom explained. A hint of a smile formed. "We have some catching up to do."

"Likewise, I want to apologize for telling you that you couldn't be a priest," Dad said. "I was sure wrong about that."

"It's all good," Emma said.

Her dad grew even more somber. "We should've done more to encourage you in your faith journey and not make you feel you had to keep it a secret."

"I'm sure you'll do better with the sibs," Emma said.

"Oh, they are," Hailey said. "We both want to be priests." As the older twin, she often spoke for her brother.

"It was my idea first," Brayden said. As the younger twin, he often tried to one-up his sister.

Emma cocked her head to peer into her brother's eyes. "Do you want to be a priest to serve the Sovereign or to impress Sarah?"

A smirk erupted on Brayden's face. "Can't I do both?"

Everyone chuckled.

After breakfast, they loaded Emma's clothes in the car and headed to the Temple for Christopher and Angie's wedding.

"What do you think about presiding over weddings?" Emma's mom asked.

"At first, it weirded me out a bit," Emma said.

"Will you do all of them?" Hailey asked.

"The priests will do most of them," Emma said.

"Does that mean I can do weddings when I become a priest?" Brayden asked.

"Possibly," Emma answered. "But that's a long way off."

"Cool!"

"Why do you want to do weddings?" Emma asked.

Brayden grinned. "So I can mess with them! You know, embarrass them and stuff."

"I don't think doing weddings will be the right place for you," Emma said.

"No way! I'll be a hit. Count on it."

Everyone else shook their heads.

Emma's mom turned toward her daughter. "On a more serious note, we want you to know how proud your father and I are of you. You've accomplished so much in such a short time. You're reforming how we practice our faith and encouraging everyone to take what they believe more seriously. Not only have you changed our family and what happens on the Temple grounds, you're changing the entire country. You're affecting the whole world."

"I'm just trying to do what the Sovereign tells me," Emma said. "And I have a team of people who do most of the work."

"Your humility is admirable," her mom said, "but next time someone compliments you, just accept it and thank them."

Emma nodded and smiled. "Thank you."

11

ROAD TRIP

After the wedding, Emma congratulated Christopher and Angie, thanking them for allowing her to be part of their celebration. Then she quietly slipped away. No one noticed. No one, that is, except for Chloe's dad, Hector Cruz.

As she headed to her room to change for the road trip with Chloe and Gabe, Mr. Cruz hustled up to her. "I know what's going on, and I'm uncomfortable with it."

"We weren't sure when to tell you," Emma said.

"Oh, I know all about it. My dad told me last night. It's a lot to wrap my mind around."

"I can't imagine how hard that would be."

"It was easier to tell Chloe her mother was dead

than to admit she had abandoned us, that she had abandoned her little girl," Hector said. "I guess that over time I began to believe that she was, in fact, dead. At least she was dead to me. To hear she's alive is unsettling."

"Gabe has had a few years to reconnect with her," Emma said, "and Chloe has had a couple of days to process it. But what about you?"

"As I said, I'm uncomfortable with it. My first thought was that I never wanted to see that woman again. But for Chloe's sake, I must try. Even though she assures me I did a great job of raising her, she so desperately wants a mom in her life too. I'll be forever grateful to your mother for stepping in at those difficult moments for a father to help his girl move into womanhood."

Emma laughed. "It's like I had a sister at my side when Mom explained things to us or took us shopping for . . . you know, for woman stuff."

"Thankfully, those days are behind us," Hector said. "What's your plan for when you meet Diane?"

Emma had never known Chloe's mother's first name. Now she did. "Chloe asked me to be there to bring peace and help avoid awkward silences."

"You'll do well at meeting both those objectives, but what's your bigger plan?"

Emma considered her words. "I feel it's important for Chloe's mom to be nearby so we can help her get her life together."

"Does that mean you plan on giving her a place to stay on the Temple grounds?"

"I think that would be a great idea," Emma said, "but she doesn't want to."

"Even though we're technically still married, under no circumstances will I let that woman into my home. It's just for me, Chloe, and my dad."

"But for Chloe's sake, at some point, you'll need to see her," Emma said.

"We'll see."

By this time, their journey had taken them to the front door of the priests' quarters, where Emma's room was. "Anything else?"

Mr. Cruz shook his head. "Just be careful, for Chloe's sake . . . and for mine."

"No problem." *But can I promise that?*

Ten minutes later Emma climbed into the backseat of Chloe's car. Chloe jumped out of the front passenger side and joined Emma in the back, much to her grandfather's dismay. "Do you intend to relegate me to the humble status of chauffeur for this outing?"

"Not at all, Gramps," Chloe said. "I just don't want Emma to have to sit by herself."

"Yet as an outcome of your action, you imply it's acceptably permissible for me to sit by myself."

Chloe snickered. "We don't want to distract you from your driving."

Gabe moved the car forward and headed to their destination. If there were no delays, the trip would take about half an hour.

"Let's pray," Emma said. "Lord, we thank you for this chance to meet Chloe's mom. May things go better this time than last. Let them connect on a deeper level. Please bless what happens and show us what to say. May we do this all for your honor. So be it."

Gabe and Chloe agreed with a hearty *amen*.

As he drove, Gabe began murmuring. Emma had seen and heard him do this many times before, but the practice confused her. He was saying words, but they made no sense. It was like he was speaking a different language, an unknown tongue.

Emma glanced at Chloe to gauge her reaction. She seemed unfazed by what her grandfather was doing. In fact, her lips moved in the same strange manner, although no words came out.

What are they doing? Emma asked this half to herself and half to the Sovereign.

The Sovereign's words formed in Emma's mind. *Why don't you ask them?*

When Gabe paused his murmuring, Emma took her chance. "Gabe, what were you doing?"

"My child, I offer up a petition from the depths of my heart for success in what we will do."

"Why don't you speak to the Sovereign like we talk to each other?" Emma said. "That's how I pray."

"Through the Divine Spirit living within us," Gabe said, "we can speak in a spiritual language. It transcends normal communication. It magnifies our prayers, even when words escape us."

"Chloe does this too," Emma said. "I've also seen Joshua, Angie, and Jennifer do the same thing. Why don't I? Is there something wrong with me?"

"I've always comprehended speaking in a spiritual language as something that flows naturally after people become filled with the Divine Spirit," Gabe said. "You have that infilling more than anyone I've ever met. Yet I'm indeed mystified as to why you presently lack this ability. Perhaps I must adjust my comprehension of this practice. I suggest you seek the Sovereign for clarity. I will do likewise."

Though Emma didn't glance at Chloe, she sensed her friend's stare. Without looking, Emma slid her hand along the seat toward Chloe. Chloe laid her hand on Emma's and clasped it.

Emma exhaled slowly, closed her eyes, and bowed her head. *Sovereign Lord,* she prayed in her mind, *why can't I do this?*

Emma waited for the Sovereign's response. Nothing.

Did I do something wrong? Are you displeased with me? Again, Emma waited for the Sovereign's words. At last they came.

I am most pleased with you, my child. Our relationship is special. Unique, I dare say. Our conversation is so rich, so deep, that you don't need to talk to me in a supernatural tongue. We talk to each other just as one person talks to another.

Thank you! Emma opened her eyes and released Chloe's hand. "I have clarity."

"As do I," Gabe said. "I can confirm there is no need for you to communicate with the Sovereign using a spiritual language. You are not like the rest of us. You are more. Much more."

12

A FATEFUL VISIT

Emma, Chloe, and Gabe sat in the waiting area at the facility where Diane was staying. The building was pleasant, but plain. There was nothing special about it, but it was comfortable and clean. That's what mattered.

A volunteer approached. "Diane is ready to see you. This way, please."

Gabe went first, and Chloe followed. Emma held back. This was their meeting, and she was just there for support.

When they entered the room, Diane squirmed. Her round face was strikingly like Chloe's. There was little doubt they were related. Although Diane had mostly gray hair, hints of black remained.

What was interesting was that her shoulder-length cut was identical to her daughter's.

Diane didn't rise to greet them or invite them to sit. After pausing for a moment with indecision, they each selected a chair.

"Diane," Gabe said. "This is Chloe's best friend Emma."

Not sure what to do, Emma stood and took a step toward Diane. "I'm so excited to meet you." She extended her arm.

Diane gave her a weak smile and an even weaker handshake. When Diane looked away and sighed, Emma returned to her chair.

An uncomfortable silence followed, which Emma took as her cue. "I'm so happy Chloe could meet you and have a chance to connect."

Diane lowered her head and wiped at her eyes. "I was so excited to see her, but I didn't know how to show it." She sniffled. "I wanted so badly to hug her, but I didn't know if I should."

Emma smiled. "I don't think we can ever get too many hugs. I'm sure Chloe is ready whenever you are."

Emma gave Chloe a nod of encouragement. Her friend rose and stepped toward her mother. Chloe extended her arms. "Hug?"

Diane looked up but didn't respond. At last she stood and moved toward her daughter. Their gazes locked. Diane lifted her arms to embrace Chloe. They had barely touched when Diane gave a timid pat on Chloe's back and pulled away.

Chloe's lip trembled. Emma sensed she was about to cry.

"Wait! I can do better." Diane lunged forward and pulled her daughter close. They shared a tight embrace. Chloe's shoulders began to quake and soon Diane's did too.

After several seconds, Diane pulled away. "I was so sure you'd hate me." Diane wiped her eyes. "You had every right to, but you didn't."

"I grew up thinking my mother was dead," Chloe said, "and I was so excited to find out you weren't. Seeing you is a dream come true."

"Knowing that you don't hate me and actually want to see me is my dream too," Diane said.

Emma grabbed a nearby box of tissues and offered it to both women. Diane snatched a tissue, and Chloe quickly followed. Then they each returned for a second one. They both needed them.

Chloe moved to an open couch and sat. She looked up at Diane and patted the cushion next to her. Diane joined her. Chloe shifted closer and grabbed her hand. "I forgive you for leaving us when I was little. I love you and want you in my life. And I'm willing to wait for however long it will take for you to be ready."

Diane raised Chloe's hand to her mouth and kissed it. "That's what I want too, but I'm not sure I'll ever be ready. I had gone six months without a drink, but last month I faltered. Again. As soon as I beat this addiction for good, I'll be ready. But not until then."

Emma looked at Diane in the spiritual realm. The woman had a faint lime green color to her spirit, the same shade as her daughter's but just not as bright. Not nearly so.

When another silence fell upon the room, Emma pushed forward. "Diane, have you put your faith in the Sovereign? Do you believe?"

"Gabriel has helped me take a few steps forward," Diane said. "Yet it's been hard for me to accept the Sovereign's mercy and grace, to believe that anyone could love me after all I've done."

"The Sovereign can help you beat your addiction," Emma said. "Accept that you can't do it on your own. Seek the Lord for strength. Though you are weak, then you will be strong."

"That's what Gabriel has told me. Many times.

Yet when I take my eyes off the Sovereign, that's when I fail."

Chloe looked at Emma. "Will you do for her what you did for me? It made all the difference in my life."

Though Emma wanted to impart the Sovereign's Divine Spirit into Diane, just as she had done for Chloe, Emma sensed the woman wasn't yet ready. "When it's the right time, I certainly will."

"I heartily concur," Gabe said.

When silence again threatened to overtake them, Emma took the lead. "Shall we go for a walk?" Emma stood. So did Chloe.

Diane sniffed. "I'd like that." She stood too.

Gabe didn't. Emma realized it was because he intended to pray for them as they walked. When she gave him a nod of approval, his lips gyrated as he prayed to the Sovereign using his spiritual language.

Though the facility had little in the way of land-scaping, a walking path surrounded it. The trio headed there. Wide enough for three people, Chloe walked on her mother's right, while Emma edged up to Diane's left.

"The Sovereign offers grace," Emma said. "We need to offer ourselves that same grace."

"But how do I do that?" Diane asked.

The answer came to Emma. "It requires time, prayer, and encouragement from others."

"Some days I pray a lot," Diane said. "But then I'll go several days and not even think about it."

"Regular prayer is a habit to form," Emma said. "I pray throughout my day as needed, but I always pray just before I go to sleep each night. That's the best time for me. Chloe prays each morning as she begins her day. Find what works for you and form a habit."

Diane chuckled quietly. "I think it's best for me to begin *and* end my day with prayer. Thanks for the suggestion. Please encourage me to form that habit."

"If only you had a phone," Chloe said, "then I could text you."

"I have a phone," Diane said, "but it's a basic plan with just voice and text, no data."

"I forgot that Grandpa's been texting you." Chloe pulled out her phone. "What's your number?"

"I don't remember it but will give it to you when we get back to my room."

"Another option," Emma said, "is for you to come back with us. We have a room where you can stay on the Temple grounds. You'll be able to see

Chloe every day. Gabe and I will be there too. We can all encourage you to develop good spiritual practices. And you'll have plenty of time to read and study the Holy Text."

"I don't have a copy," Diane said. "A social worker sideloaded a file of the Holy Text on my phone, but that's not how I learn. I need to read from a real book."

"We'll get you one," Emma said. "And let us know when you'd like to come back with us. The offer is open anytime."

"I've already thought a lot about it," Diane said. "I had hoped you'd ask me again today and I'm already packed."

13

____

SUNDAY REVELATIONS

Emma's Sunday schedule was both simple and doable: she was to give the concluding blessing at each of the five services. She drove her golf cart to the ancient Temple, slipped into her robe, and waited for the service to wind down. Ezra played his zither as an ensemble of priests chanted the concluding rite.

As their final words came forth, Emma eased to the front of the Temple. "Rise to receive the benediction. Hear these words of the prophet Abdiel as recorded in History 79.146: 'May the Lord's love shine upon you, fill you with peace, and overflow with joy as you go forth to help those who hurt, proclaim the good news across the land, and restore to fellowship all who repent.' Amen."

Everyone in the packed Temple echoed their amen and streamed from the building. Many more stood outside, waiting to enter for the second service. Within minutes, people packed the space. Sitting in the front row, Ezra leaned toward Emma and whispered: "Looks like we'll need to add a third service."

Emma gave him a weak smile, knowing that a third service at the Temple would start at the same time as the first service at the Sunshine Auditorium. Then she could no longer take part in every service as the Sovereign had told her to do. They would need to talk about it—they, as in Emma and the Sovereign.

After giving the concluding blessing for the second service at the Temple, Emma changed out of her brown robe and drove to the Sunshine Auditorium to end that service. Next, she repeated it at the Jacob G. Turrum Auditorium, where she always wore her light blue robe. Once finished, she hung her robe up for next week and drove back to Sunshine Auditorium.

She hadn't made it twenty paces when the Sovereign spoke to her. *Go see Diane.*

As soon as the last service is over, Emma said in her spirit.

That will be too late, came her Lord's reply.

Emma zoomed past Sunshine Auditorium and headed straight to the Palace, where Diane was staying. Trudging toward her was Diane, with a backpack slung over her shoulder and a bag in each hand. She stopped walking when she saw Emma.

Emma pulled up next to her and stopped. "Morning, Diane."

The woman shook her head. "I shouldn't be here. It was a mistake for me to come."

"Nonsense," Emma said. "That's the devil's lies you're hearing and not the Sovereign's truth." Emma paused as she received a divine revelation. "You know that drinking won't help."

Both of Diane's bags dropped to the ground with a thud. She stared at Emma. "How did you know?"

Emma got out of the cart and placed both bags in the rear seat. "This is your home now. Let's head back."

Diane stood there as if frozen in time.

"Think of how hurt Chloe will be if you leave her . . . again. She'll be devastated."

Diane didn't move, but when she blinked, a tear leaked from her eye. "It's Hector. I'm embarrassed to see him. Ashamed. He'll never take me back. I have no reason to hope he will. It's too much to expect that he'll ever love me again."

"Don't forget, you two are still married," Emma said. "You're worrying about things that may never happen. The first step is to talk to him. I believe that will happen according to the Sovereign's perfect timing. It might be tomorrow, or it could be next year. We just don't know."

Diane gave a slight nod as she processed Emma's words.

"But if you run away, talking can't happen." Emma got back in her cart and patted the seat next to her. "Hop in. Let's take your stuff back to your room."

Without a word, Diane got in.

Once back at Diane's room in the Palace, Emma helped her unpack and put everything away. "May the Sovereign bless you as you move forward in your life," Emma prayed aloud. "And Lord, take away Diane's desire for alcohol. May she never take another drink again. Let her seek you instead."

Emma sat with Diane, but a conflict raged in her mind. *Should I stay with Diane and skip the last service, or should I leave Diane so I can do what's expected of me?*

Why not do both? came the Sovereign's answer.

Emma paused as she wondered just how to do that. Soon she figured it out. "Diane, will you go with me so we can catch the end of the last service?"

The woman nodded, and the pair headed out. Once there, Emma parked her cart behind the auditorium and guided Diane inside. Reaching her dressing room, the final number was about to end. Emma wouldn't have time to change into her pink robe. She slowed her pace and turned toward Diane. "I need to give the benediction in a few seconds. You can wait in my dressing room. Then we'll go to lunch."

Diane gave a single nod, and Emma rushed toward the stage.

She inhaled deeply, prayed for the Sovereign's favor, and reached the first step as the song ended. Slowing her pace, she climbed the stairs with a reverent slowness. The choir parted, and she stepped toward the dais. It was the first time she'd ever stood before the people at a Sunday service without wearing a rope. Emma sensed the Sovereign didn't care what she wore, and she hoped the people there would offer her grace.

As she reached her mark, she raised both arms. "Rise to receive the benediction." Then it came to her. Divine revelation flooded her mind in an instant. It was a tune—the tune—a heavenly harmony to accompany the words of the Holy Text. Her prayers—and the priests' prayers—for supernatural insight were answered. The timing was perfect.

Without giving it another thought or having time to second-guess what she was about to do, Emma opened her mouth and began to sing. Her rich alto flowed forth with ease, strong and confident. "May the Lord's love shine upon you, fill you with peace, and overflow with joy as you go forth to help those who hurt, proclaim the good news across the land, and restore to fellowship all who repent."

Emma lowered her arms, her face beaming. "Have a great week. See you next Sunday." She waved goodbye and left the stage as the people exited the auditorium.

Diane stood at the side of the stage, wide-eyed at what had just happened.

Chloe rushed up to her mom and wrapped her arms around her. "I've been praying for you and am so glad you could make it."

Chloe's grandpa walked up behind Chloe, but her dad held back. After several seconds, he took a halting step forward and then another. As if moving in slow motion, he inched toward his estranged wife.

Diane spotted his tentative approach. Their eyes fixed on each other.

"Diane," he said. "It's been a while."

"Hector," she responded.

That was it. No one said anything more.

Emma broke the tension. "Let's go to my dressing room for some privacy." She pointed to the open door and led the way. Everyone followed. Reaching the door, Emma stepped aside and gestured for them to enter. Chloe walked in first and then Gabe. Diane followed. Hector walked up last. "I wasn't planning on ever talking to her again," he whispered to Emma, "but after hearing the words you sang in your benediction, I knew I had to."

"May the Sovereign bless you for listening and obeying." Emma eased the door shut and left.

Sovereign, she prayed in her spirit, *bless them and what they say. Help them reconcile. So be it.*

14

MONDAY MEETINGS

Monday morning, Emma sat in a grand conference room at the offices of the Prison Oversight Authority in the capital. Michael presented the details of their proposed plan to overhaul the prison facility in Lakeview County.

Since Emma knew what he would say, her mind drifted. Yesterday, the flight to the capital had been uneventful, and she finished her Monday's homework before they landed. That evening she had an extra hour to study the Holy Text. She also took time to sit in the Sovereign's presence and recharge her spirit. It was a powerful end to her week, and she was ready to embrace all the opportunities before her.

As Michael spoke, the staff leaned forward in their seats, responding to his words with smiles and giving him nods of approval. "In conclusion," he said, "our goal in all this is to introduce a new way of integrating prisoners back into the world. We want to prepare them to become productive members of society and to equip them with new life skills, so they don't return to prison." He looked up and then added, "Thank you for your time and attention. Are you ready to move forward?"

"Overall," the director said, "I appreciate your vision for change, innovative perspective, and anticipated outcomes. My only concern is the religious component in this. While I will not insist you remove it completely, can you deemphasize it?"

"Faith is a critical factor in what we intend to accomplish," Michael said. "If the prisoners are sorry for what they have done, spiritual repentance should follow. A firm faith will provide a foundation for them to move forward and realize the outcomes we seek."

"I can appreciate that," the director said, "but how will you address the needs of someone who is agnostic?"

"Our program will not be a good fit for that individual," Michael said. "I'm not saying they can't be rehabilitated, but that will need to come from a different program. We'll screen them out in the application process. That way we can ensure the faith component of our plan will remain intact and not be a stumbling block."

"How soon can you start?" the director asked. "Is the beginning of next year rushing things?"

Emma couldn't remain quiet any longer. "How about the beginning of next month?" Everyone turned toward her. She stood and walked to the podium, moving next to Michael.

The twinkle in his eye confirmed he agreed with her timetable.

"Let's not delay things," Emma said. "The longer we wait, the harder it will be to reopen the prison. We have two priests ready to move to the area, and I suspect two more will be ready soon. Also, most of the former prison staff is still looking for work. I want to hire them as quickly as possible and help restore the local economy."

"Are you sure you can get going by the beginning of next month?" the director asked.

Emma considered her words before speaking, but Michael spoke first. "Frankly, I'm surprised she didn't say next week."

When he grinned, everyone in the room laughed.

"In all seriousness," Michael said, "the Sovereign has blessed Emma in all that she has set out to do. I fully expect that to continue at the Lakeview County facility. With Emma's passion and vision, next month is certainly doable."

"You have a lot riding on this," the director said. "I don't want you to risk ruining this opportunity with a timetable that's too aggressive."

Emma smiled. "That's why I said next month and not next week."

"A last question," the director said. "Emma, what about lifers? We don't want someone with a life sentence being accepted into your program and then released back into society."

This was something Emma and Michael hadn't considered. As her mind scrambled for an answer, clarity came from the Sovereign.

"Great question," Emma said. "The focus is on first-time and nonviolent offenders, but everyone who repents can be in our program. This includes people with life sentences. But instead of releasing them back into society, we'll release them back into the prison system."

Emma gave her audience time to process what

she had said. "That way they can take what they've learned from us and share it with other prisoners in facilities across the country. Though they'll never leave prison, they can help others get ready to move on with their lives once they're released."

The director stood and walked over to Emma and Michael. "You've addressed my remaining concerns, and I'm ready to move forward." He handed them a folder. "I've already signed the agreement you sent. Please proceed as you see fit."

Emma, Michael, and Fred celebrated their successful meeting as they awaited lunch. The Sovereign brought Emma's attention to a distin-guished-looking woman who entered the restaurant. Though she carried herself with confidence, a pronounced scowl marked her as a woman who was not approachable.

Introduce yourself, the Sovereign instructed Emma.

Emma rose from her chair and then sat down again. "Frederick, do you recognize that woman?

"I don't. Should I?"

"Just checking. The Sovereign told me to go talk to her."

"This should be interesting." Fred's eyes twinkled. "What are you waiting for?"

Emma stood again. This time she moved toward the woman, her heart thumping in her chest. Worry filled her that she was about to make a complete fool of herself. "Hi! I'm Emma Barlow." Emma extended her hand toward the frowning woman.

A well-groomed man in a black suit abruptly stepped between the two of them. He pushed Emma away. "Ms. Cartwright is not to be interrupted under any circumstances."

"It's okay, Luther," the woman said. "I recognize this young lady. She is the High Priestess."

The man stepped back. "My apologies. To both of you." He tipped his head down once and backed away.

"Luther is my bodyguard," Ms. Cartwright explained to Emma. "I pay him to protect me, and he does his job with excellence."

"I'm sorry for interrupting you," Emma said, "but I felt prompted to introduce myself."

A pleased smile replaced the woman's frown. "A prompting from the Sovereign?"

"Yes."

Ms. Cartwright sighed. "I so wish I could hear

the Sovereign speak to me, but alas that has not occurred."

Emma wondered if that was why she was supposed to talk to the woman, to teach her how to hear from the Sovereign.

No. The supernatural words formed in Emma's mind. *At least not today.*

What should I do? Emma silently asked the Sovereign.

Invite her to join you for lunch.

Emma's pulse raced. She worried she was about to pass out. "If you don't have other plans, would you like to join us for lunch?" Emma tipped her head toward the table where Fred and Michael sat watching them.

"Of course I have plans," the woman snapped. Then she relaxed. "But I wonder if the Sovereign has a better plan. I came here to conclude a multi-million dollar transaction, but while en route, they called to reschedule. I won't give them a second chance to buy my building."

Emma gestured toward her table, and Ms. Cartwright paraded toward it. When Emma beckoned Luther to follow, he shook his head. "I'll eat later."

Emma followed Ms. Cartwright and introduced

her new friend to Fred and Michael, who stood to receive her.

A waiter rushed over with table service. "Would you like your usual, Ms. Cartwright?"

"Yes, Samuel. Thank you."

Though Emma wanted to get to know Ms. Cartwright, the woman was more interested in listening to what Emma had to say. Emma shared about their meeting with the Prison Oversight Authority and their plans for the Lakeview facility.

"I have a wayward nephew incarcerated for some youthful indiscretions. Perhaps your program might be a good fit for him."

"We're certainly open to consider him," Michael said.

"We're also here to look for space to hold a Sunday service," Emma added. "During the week we can minister to the senators and their staff."

"Given that my lunch meeting fell through, this information is interesting," Ms. Cartwright said. "Most interesting."

When their food arrived, Emma thanked the Sovereign for their meal and asked for blessings on their conversation. They ate, and they talked. Ms. Cartwright peppered Emma with questions about faith, the Sovereign, and the Holy Text.

She paused eating and looked intently at Emma. "Until a few months ago—when you encouraged us to read the Holy Text—I had never even considered it. I'd been taught that ordinary people shouldn't read it and couldn't even understand it. You opened my eyes to what could be and deepened my faith in the process."

As they finished their meal and their conversation, Ms. Cartwright signaled for the waiter. "Please put these meals on my tab, Samuel."

Fred held up the palm of his hand. "Permit me to pay."

"Nonsense. I shan't hear of it," Ms. Cartwright said. She pulled a business card from her purse and slid it toward Fred. "Call my office this afternoon and set up an appointment for tomorrow. I have a building that would be ideal for your services, and I have the money to help you get started. We'll make this happen." She stood and left, with her bodyguard trailing her.

Marveling over their lunch and what Ms. Cartwright had offered, the trio headed to the prison. But the Prime Minister refused to meet with Emma.

15

THE VIP DONOR CLUB

Emma trudged behind Fred and Michael as they walked toward their rental car. Dejected, she slid into the backseat. As Fred started the car, Michael glanced back at Emma. "Don't focus on one disappointment. Instead, celebrate that things went well with the Prison Oversight Authority. We even walked away with a signed agreement, which we hadn't expected to happen today."

Fred also turned around. "Additionally, you connected with Ms. Cartwright. I'm most optimistic of our chances to move forward quickly to establish our base here in the capital. Without your supernatural perception, that never would've happened."

"I'm happy about both of those things," Emma

said. "But my goal was to meet with the Prime Minister. I failed."

"As I recall," Fred responded, "you said the Sovereign told you to *try* to meet with the Prime Minister. You did indeed try. You were obedient. Embrace that."

"You're right," Emma said, "but I still feel like I failed."

"I suggest you get the Sovereign's perspective on that," Fred said.

But Emma didn't need to. She already knew how her Lord felt. She had done what she had been told to do, and that's what mattered. Emma closed her eyes, inhaled deeply, and let the Sovereign's peace fill her. Even so, it would take a while for her to move past her disappointment over the Prime Minister refusing to see her.

Emma opened her eyes and looked out the window, marveling at the whooshing traffic that surrounded them and the constant noise that never let up. "I could never drive in a place like this."

"As you gain experience behind the wheel," Fred said, "your confidence will grow, and you'll develop the skill to navigate challenging situations."

"Why did you rent a car this time instead of hiring a driver like last week?" Emma asked.

"I briefly considered renting a car last time as well," Fred said, "but given our tight schedule, and that parking near the Senate building is next to impossible, I determined that hiring a driver was our best solution."

"So just because you could've driven last week," Emma said, "doesn't mean that was the right thing to do."

"It would've saved money," Fred said, "but it also would've caused a lot of stress and possibly made us late a time or two."

"I'm curious," Michael said. "When you said there were possibly four priests ready to move to Lakeview County, did you get excited and exaggerate, or is there something I'm not aware of? I only know of two."

Emma snickered. "I sense you would like to move there and implement what you proposed. I also perceive that Jerry would be more than happy to move back there as well."

"Indeed, Jerry and I have discussed such a possibility. Yet we have a year of training to complete first before we become priests."

"Maybe you could do your training remotely," Emma said. "Study half a day and work the other half. You and Jerry could have your own little classroom and connect online with the other priests back at the Temple. I think it could work."

"I agree," Fred said. "But let's first check with Elizabeth, as lead instructor, and Mark, as chief of priests, to get their input, but I'm behind it."

Emma pulled out her laptop. "I'm going to send the Prime Minister a letter. Although prisoners can't access the internet, I can email a message to the prison for her. They'll print it out and deliver it."

"Perhaps your letter will have the impact you desire," Fred said.

"I pray it will," Emma said. "I also pray that the Prime Minister will repent and trust the Sovereign."

Emma asked the Lord for guidance in what to write and began typing. She completed her draft, proofread it, and sent it. As she closed her laptop, her phone chirped. So did Fred's. It was a group text.

Emma read the message. "Christopher wants to know if either of us has any info about a VIP Donor Club. One of our top contributors contacted us today to confirm this week's schedule."

Fred groaned. "I suspect it's something Barney set up. But how will we figure out what it is without being able to talk to him? We'd certainly look foolish if we asked the contributor to explain it to us."

"I could visit Barney tomorrow in prison and ask. But can we wait that long?" Emma asked. "He said he'd only talk to me, but Gabe is on his visitor list. Maybe Gabe can go today."

"Since you'll soon be on a plane and not able to communicate, I suggest we have Christopher work with Gabe on this," Fred said. "That will also help prepare Christopher to take over for me when I leave for the capital."

Emma composed the message to Christopher on her phone and sent it. "There might also be some files on Barney's work computer. Lane has the login and can check."

"An excellent suggestion," Fred said. "Will you also relay that idea to Christopher? And ask him to let us know what he finds out."

Emma sent that message too.

Fred pulled up to the passenger drop-off area. Saying goodbye, Emma and Michael got out, grabbed their luggage, and walked into the airport. They got in line. A long line. Emma braced herself for a lengthy wait. It was good that they had gotten there early.

A smiling airport official approached Emma. "We are pleased to see you today, High Priestess," he said. "Please follow me."

Emma glanced at Michael. He shrugged.

"Both of you," the man said. "You can skip this line, have expedited security, and board whenever you wish."

Emma was ready to tell the man she didn't want special treatment when she recalled Fred's advice to her last week about this very topic: Be thankful when it happens, don't be upset when it doesn't, and most importantly, never expect it.

"Thank you," Emma said.

"Though we can upgrade you to first class," the man said, "there's only one seat available."

"I appreciate the offer," Emma said, "but I'm happy to sit in coach with Michael."

In no time at all, Emma and Michael had boarded the jet. Once Emma stowed her luggage, she settled down to read Christopher's update. "Can confirm that Barney set up VIP Donor Club as a perk for million-dollar-a-year contributors. Ten couples are part of it. They get to spend four days with us, staying at the Palace and experiencing life on the Temple grounds. Besides our needing to feed them, there's a gala celebration this Friday."

Then a follow-up message said, "We're also supposed to pick them up at the airport with a limo. The bad news is that with Aurora and Diane both living in the Palace, we only have eight rooms left for the ten couples."

Emma prayed for insight. It quickly came, and she texted Christopher: "Please explain the situation to Aurora and Diane, apologize to them for me, and ask if they'd be willing to move into one of the two rooms connected to mine. It will only be for a few days."

She was about to put her phone away when she realized she wasn't finished. "Also, ask Topher if he can score a limo for us and return to being a chauffeur for a bit."

She powered down her phone and put it away. *Thank you, Sovereign,* Emma prayed silently. *Show me how to deal with the VIP Donor Club. May the money they give be for the right reasons.*

16

BARNEY'S BABY STEP

At lunch the next day, Emma updated her team on the success of Monday's trip to the capital—of the signed agreement with the Prison Oversight Authority and the connection with Ms. Cartwright. Without a hint of shame, she also shared that she had attempted to meet with the Prime Minister but couldn't.

Then Christopher gave his update about the VIP Donor Club. "Here's what we've been able to piece together: First, the club comprises ten couples. Each couple gave one million last year. This means that together they accounted for half of our donations. With increased giving from other sources, that projects to only about a third of our donations for this year. Still, we need to make sure we don't lose the support of a single one of them."

"I'm more concerned that if they give, they do it for the right reasons," Emma said. "Even if none of them give another cent, I have faith the Sovereign will give us what we need."

Christopher stiffened at Emma's response but continued his update. "They'll arrive on Thursday. Topher will rent a limo and pick them up at the airport throughout the day. They'll stay in the Palace through Sunday. The focus of their time here is a gala Friday night. The goal is for them to recommit their giving for the coming year. Through it all, we need to keep them entertained, engaged, and impressed by all that we do."

"I'll meet with Barney this afternoon," Emma said. "Maybe I can learn more."

"We have much to do between now and Thursday," Christopher added. "Fortunately, Frederick will be back tomorrow and can run point, but I'll get things started today."

When Christopher ended the meeting, Emma and Gabe drove to the prison.

The woman at the prison perked up as soon as Emma walked in. "Welcome back." She handed the sign-in sheet to Emma. "Because of his assault on your last visit, Barney Clark may no longer have direct contact with visitors. You'll be meeting with him in our secure visitor section. A sheet of bullet-proof glass will separate you from him. There's a telephone so you can talk to each other."

"Thanks, but that isn't necessary," Emma said. "I'm sure it won't happen again."

"Regardless," the woman said, "we have proto-cols we must follow." She escorted Emma to another door and opened it. "Sit wherever you like. He'll arrive shortly."

The room had three stations, each with a chair, a shelf, and a phone. A glass partition separated the visitor stations from the prisoner section. Emma sat at the middle of the three, assuming that would be Barney's preference.

The door on the opposite side of the room opened. A guard escorted Barney in. When Barney moved toward the station where Emma sat, the guard stood by the door, with crossed arms and a don't-mess-with-me glare.

As Barney approached, Emma flashed a friendly smile and waved. His visage in the spiritual realm was no longer black, but dark gray. This was a good sign.

Barney sat and picked up the phone's handset

on his side of the glass. Emma picked up hers and brought it to her ear.

"Hi, Emma," Barney said. "I'm sure you have questions about the VIP Donor Club. I am ready and able to assist. Know that I only told Gabe the basics last night and held back the best information for you."

"The whole thing took us by surprise," Emma said.

"Don't you fret. The main thing is to wine and dine them. I'm sure with a little effort and a lot of flattery, they'll all recommit for another year. Let me go through the list and tell you the hot buttons of each couple and what motivates them to give."

This wasn't the information Emma wanted to hear. She shook her head. "Let's talk about you."

Barney recoiled. "I've been grooming these relationships for years. Don't get careless and jeopardize all that I've established."

"Did you get your copy of the Holy Text I left for you?"

"I did. Thank you." Barney tipped his head to the side. "But if you could get the Holy Text to me, certainly you could get them to let you bring Montgomery to see me."

"Not going to try." Emma felt bad for being

harsh, but then she relaxed. "Have you been reading it?"

"I have. I'm finally beginning to understand some of it. It's like I was blind to its words before, but now I see with more clarity."

"What are you learning?" Emma asked.

"That I need to trust the Sovereign by faith. That I can't earn my salvation."

"Excellent! Have you done that?"

"I have indeed . . . at least I'm trying to. It's hard to undo sixteen years of rebellion in a single moment."

The dark gray of Barney's spiritual countenance lightened.

"To show that I'm a changed man, I'll donate half my remaining money to the Temple. That's over five million. You can have most of the rest once my trial is over. But I'll hold some back just in case."

Emma shook her head. "Don't think for a moment you can buy your salvation."

"I'm not trying to buy it. I'm trying to prove it."

Emma sensed his sincerity. It was the first time she truly believed anything he had said.

"I accept that I'll never leave prison for the rest of my life," Barney said. "I've made my peace with it and need to learn how to serve the Sovereign in some way from behind bars."

Emma perked up. "We've been meeting with the Prison Oversight Authority to take over the facility in Lakeview County. We'll help prisoners get ready for their release and give them training—all anchored in the Holy Text—so that they don't return."

"Can I be part of it?"

"You can apply," Emma said. "But the goal for people with life sentences isn't to release them back into society. It's to return them to the prison system so they can work with other inmates."

"When my training is done, will I be able to return to this facility?" Barney asked.

"Why do you want to come back here?"

Barney looked away for a moment. Bringing his hand to his chin, he looked directly at Emma. "Because you're here."

Emma raised her eyebrows.

"We've had a rocky relationship," he said, "but that's on me. You've always offered me grace and shown me the Sovereign's love. In truth, you're an important part of my life."

Emma didn't know what to say, so she kept quiet.

Barney continued. "I feel you're the closest thing I have to family. If I return here to work with the prisoners, I'll know you'll be nearby and there's a chance to see you on occasion."

"It can all start when you give your life to the Sovereign," Emma said. "Take a baby step of faith and start today."

"I want to believe." Then Barney hung his head. "But I have doubts."

Emma transferred the handset to her left and placed her right palm on the glass. Barney brought his hand to align with hers. "Sovereign Lord," Emma said, "grow Barney's faith and remove his doubt."

Physically, Barney blinked several times, and a tear dripped from his eye. Spiritually, his gray appearance morphed into a pale baby blue.

Emma was about to cry too. At last, he was ready. "Barney Clark, may you receive the Divine Spirit to live within you and direct all that you do."

Joy radiated from his face, and tears flowed from his eyes. He opened his mouth to speak, but no words came out. He hung up the handset in its cradle and mouthed the words, "Thank you."

17

PREPARING FOR THE DONORS

By Wednesday evening, everything was in place for the VIP Donor Club, whose members would arrive throughout the day on Thursday. Fred had worked hard to pull everything together, fretting over every detail.

Topher did indeed line up a limo, but it came with its own driver. Even though he had his chauffeur's license, they prohibited him from driving. Christopher had assigned a priest and female employee to greet each couple when they arrived. The task was to escort each couple around the Temple grounds, answer questions, and work to ensure they'd continue their contributions for another year. A secondary goal was to protect Emma's time and shield her from interruptions.

Aside from the Friday night gala, donor club members would eat in the cafeteria, sitting at a special VIP table reserved for them.

The gala was the most important part of the four days. It would take place in the banquet room in the Palace. Staff would serve the guests an eight-course meal. A women's trio would provide entertainment. Fred would be the main speaker and ask for their pledges for another year.

Emma would give a small presentation, too, which Fred wanted her to practice so he could provide feedback.

"I'm going to say what the Sovereign tells me to say at that time," Emma explained. "So there's nothing to practice."

Fred clamped his lips and shook his head. "I'm most uncomfortable with this." But he didn't pursue it further.

Emma prayed aloud. "Lord, bless Fred's work and prepare each couple to give what you prompt them to give. May we do this for your glory and your kingdom. Amen."

Guests arrived throughout the day on Thursday, and Emma went through her normal schedule. She trusted Fred had everything under control and was determined not to interfere. The only time she saw the VIP Donor Club members was at meals, with them sitting at their special table. They mostly ate in silence. Their stern faces and closed postures made them look unapproachable.

Emma was glad she'd only have to interact with them during the gala.

After school on Friday morning, Emma went to the cafeteria for lunch to meet with her leadership team as usual. But the Sovereign had a different idea. *Go talk to the VIP Donor Club.*

Emma strolled up to their table in the cafeteria. She relaxed her posture and smiled. "Hi," she said with a wave. "How's everyone doing?"

They all looked at her and scowled. At last, one of them spoke. "Not well."

Emma scrunched her eyebrows and cocked her head. "Why? What's wrong?"

"As a group, we're all quite perturbed at how we've been treated. We don't like that you've ignored us. We paid for access but aren't receiving it. Frankly, I'm contemplating demanding a refund."

Emma whispered a panicked prayer in her mind. *Help!* She stepped closer to the table. "I'm so sorry you're disappointed. My team has worked hard to serve you. What can I do to make things right?"

"It may be too late for that," one woman said. "Since we all need to eat, we'll stick around for the gala tonight, but we're leaving as soon as it's over."

Fred rushed up to the other end of the table. "Please excuse the High Priestess. She's not been feeling well."

As the donors turned to look at Fred, Christopher rushed up to Emma and pushed her toward her normal table in the cafeteria.

"I think I need to meet with them," Emma whispered.

"Let Fred handle the situation. Don't give it another thought."

But Emma did. She thought about it all afternoon. She prayed just as often. And she asked the Sovereign for wisdom.

18

DEALING WITH THE DONORS

The gala got off to a rocky start when Zoe showed up to help serve the meal.

Fred shook his head. "I don't want her here," he hissed to Emma.

"I do," Emma said.

"Her tattoos and piercings are inappropriate for this setting," Fred said. "The donors must not see her."

"Though I don't know why, she needs to be here," Emma countered. "I'm sure of it."

"This couldn't be going any worse." Fred stomped away.

But things did get worse. The trio couldn't make it, leaving them with no entertainment and a half-hour gap in the schedule.

"I have an idea," Emma said.

Fred shook his head.

Emma marched to the stage in the banquet room. She stepped up to the microphone and scanned the group. When they saw her standing there, a hush rippled across the room.

"I hope you're enjoying this delicious meal," Emma said. "We had planned for a women's trio to sing as we served dessert, but they had to cancel at the last moment. I'm going to do my best to fill in. But since I haven't practiced, I ask for grace."

Emma closed her eyes and exhaled slowly as she prayed for peace and asked for direction on what songs to sing. The room became completely still. She inhaled deeply and opened her eyes, a smile bursting forth. Singing a cappella, she launched into the finale of last year's school musical, where she had the lead. Her rich alto filled the space, reverberating off the walls. The stiff crowd relaxed. Some even smiled.

Encouraged by their reaction and bolstered by the Sovereign's approval, Emma moved directly to a second musical number and then a third. After that, she sang two of their most revered hymns. But having no more hymns she felt confident to sing, she shifted to a series of their faith's contemporary songs and popular choruses. She knew them much better. By the time she concluded her final number, everyone was gazing at her in wide-eyed appreciation, mesmerized by her performance.

Emma was done, but the Sovereign wasn't. *Sing the benediction like you did at Sunday's service,* the Sovereign said.

Emma did. When finished, she gave a slight bow and then lifted her right hand heavenward. The crowd erupted in applause and stood to show their appreciation.

Speak from your heart, came the Sovereign's silent instructions.

Emma lowered her arm partway, extended her hand to them, and tipped her head down once. She mouthed the words thank you. She patted her chest and smiled. "Thank you."

As the applause tapered off, the people sat. But they kept their eyes fixed on her.

"I don't like asking for money," Emma said. "I never have and won't start tonight." She smiled at the apparent irony of what she was about to say. "Yet we all know that this banquet is to get your pledge of financial support for the coming year. But frankly, I don't care."

Several people gasped, and everyone's smiles

vanished. From the back of the room, Fred waved frantically for her to stop. She didn't.

"Why are you giving? What's your motivation? Are you doing it for a tax write-off? To tell others you spent a few nights in the Palace? Or maybe to buy access and influence?" She shook her head. "Those are lousy reasons."

Fred marched over to the sound booth, making frantic gestures to its operator.

Emma pressed forward. "I want you to examine why you donate." But her mic went dead, and only the people closest to her heard the last half of her sentence.

Yet all of Emma's experience in performances had taught her how to project. She took a deep breath and spoke from her diaphragm, loud enough for everyone to hear: "I want you to examine why you donate. The Sovereign wants us to give generously and cheerfully. The Holy Text says so. If you don't want to give, don't. If you can't do it joyfully, keep your money."

One woman stood. "I've never been treated so shamefully in my entire life." She marched out of the room, and her husband followed.

Another man cleared his throat and rose. "I too have had enough. I refuse to endure any more insults." He stomped out of the room with his wife in tow.

A third woman stood. "Come, Harold. We're leaving too."

Harold shook his head. A stare-down resulted.

She glared at him with the most commanding of scowls.

At last he stood. "We'll discuss this in private." He left, and she followed.

Zoe stopped her cleanup efforts and snuck out after them, easing the doors shut as she left. Muffled sounds came from behind the closed doors.

Emma continued speaking, despite Fred's frantic gestures for her to stop. "You all have commitment cards in front of you. Don't fill them out tonight. Wait until you're ready—or don't. Ask the Sovereign if you should give this year. Then ask how much. Donate what you feel led to give, not a penny more and not a penny less."

Fred stomped from the room.

Emma scanned the group. Most of them seemed to have recovered from the shock of her words and were contemplating what she was saying. "We've made a lot of positive changes here in the past few months, attendance is way up, and people are growing in their faith like never before. I hope you are too. We're also expanding our outreach. We have much more planned."

Emma paused as she waited for more of the Sovereign's direction. "Though this will take money, it doesn't depend on you. With you or without you, I know the Sovereign will provide all the money we need."

Emma considered her concluding words. "I challenge you to ask the Sovereign what you should give, be it the same amount, more, or nothing."

Emma stepped away from the microphone but then returned. "And if you decide to stick around, let's hang out tomorrow." She waved goodbye and left.

19

DIANE'S ADVENTURE

Emma strolled to her room, marveling at how unexpectedly the evening had gone. Overall, she felt good about what had happened.

Though Chloe had left for the weekend, Emma's temporary roommates of Aurora and Diane would be there. While each had their own space, Emma opened the door to find them both sitting in her room, engaged in animated conversation.

Aurora looked up. "How did it go?"

Emma chuckled. "I gave the donors a lot to think about. Frederick is mad at me, and the Sovereign is pleased."

"Sounds like we missed some drama."

Emma sat to join them. "In two days, they'll be gone, and you can both return to your own rooms in the Palace."

"I'm not sure I want to," Diane said. "I'm used to being around people. I was lonely in a room by myself. Having Chloe here last night was a real bonus."

"I liked it too," Aurora said. "It reminded me of my sorority days at college. Those were good times."

"It doesn't look like we'll be able to spend much time together tomorrow," Emma apologized. "It seems I have some work to do with the donors . . . at least those who stick around. I promised them we could hang out."

"No worries," Aurora said. "I've got plenty of work to do around here. The welcome center construction is ahead of schedule and needs my attention to keep it that way. The dorm room renovations are on track, and I want to make sure that continues. Then, I must prepare for next week. All that to say, I won't be around much either."

Emma and Aurora looked at Diane. "It seems I have plans too. Hector, Chloe, and Gabe are moving into their new house tomorrow. All of Chloe's friends—your disciples, I think you call them—are going to help. So am I. Hector didn't seem so keen on the idea, but Chloe was thrilled. Please pray that everything works out."

"How's it been going with you?" Emma asked Diane.

"Should I leave so the two of you can talk?" Aurora asked.

Diane shook her head. "You already know what I'm going to say." Then she turned to Emma. "Last Sunday—after a bit of yelling and a lot of tears—Hector and I reached an uneasy truce. He knows it's important for me to be part of Chloe's life and pledged to not stand in the way. Yet he still has trouble even looking me in the eye. I'm sure he sees only disappointment and broken promises. We've texted a bit throughout the week, but that's been it. Though I really want to help tomorrow, I'm a little nervous too. Actually, a lot nervous."

"How have your days here been going?" Emma asked.

"I've been meeting with Olivia every day," Diane said. "She's an amazing counselor and has helped me so much. I now know what I need to work on. We have a plan. I've also spent a lot of time with Gabe and some priests, learning about faith and the Holy Text."

When Diane paused, Emma gave her an encouraging nod to continue.

The woman resumed. "In my spare time, I've been helping Beatrice at the communication center. It's so invigorating to do something productive. But the best part is getting to spend time with my daughter. I've got a lot of lost ground to make up for, and I don't want to miss another moment of her life."

"What's your next step with Chloe's dad?" Emma asked Diane.

"I'm working on writing an apology to Hecter," Diane said. "How he responds will determine what I do next. I'm also looking for ways to show him how sorry I am. I want to prove that I'm changed and can be trusted to spend time with Chloe."

Emma prayed for both women, and they retired to their own rooms. Emma took Montgomery for a walk, studied the Holy Text, and went to sleep. Soon it was morning.

Emma and Montgomery headed out early for breakfast. She paused at the priests' table and asked them to pray for her time with the donors. Then she got her food and waited at the VIP table.

The couples trickled in. As they arrived, Emma —along with Montgomery's infectious tail wagging —worked to connect with each of them. She apologized for not having spent time with them. Most of them understood, realizing it was Fred who had kept her away from them.

Emma knew that the first two couples who had stormed from the banquet last night had left in a huff. Topher and Christopher had each driven one couple to the hotel next to the airport. Seven couples sat at the table with Emma. She wondered about the last pair.

They soon arrived. The husband, Harold, surveyed the group. "Let me apologize for the drama we caused last night. I'm sorry for further disrupting the banquet."

The other couples assured him everything was okay.

"Emma gave us much to think about last night," Harold said, "but it took a while for my wife and me to get on the same page."

Harold's wife smiled. "Thankfully, the waitress calmed me down. Her name's Zoe. She listened and then talked sense into me. Without her help, we'd have been gone too. Or at least I would have been." The woman chuckled. "Zoe reminds me so much of our daughter—opinionated and blunt—along with too many tattoos and piercings."

"The important thing," Harold said, "is that we're still here and have our commitment card filled out." He handed an envelope to Emma.

"Thank you!"

In a rush of activity, the other couples passed in their commitment cards too. Soon Emma held eight envelopes. She scanned the table, intent to make eye contact with each person. "Thank you for taking the time to listen to the Sovereign. May our Lord bless your commitment and multiply your contributions."

She spotted Topher across the cafeteria, having just finished his breakfast. Emma excused herself for a moment and delivered the commitment cards to the accountant. Then she hustled back to the donors. "Before we get started on our day, do you have any questions?"

Did they ever.

Montgomery jumped onto Emma's lap when she sat. She answered every question the best she could. She wasn't sure who was the bigger hit, her or her puppy. But it was all good.

Then she took them on a tour of the Temple grounds, introducing them to staff and priests, explaining the recent changes, and sharing her vision for the facility. They took a break for a leisurely lunch and then resumed the tour. She spent extra time at the ancient Temple and the two auditoriums, talking at length about the Sunday services at each location, what they emphasized, and how they were different.

Emma judged the day as a success. The couples connected with her and with each other. They also had several meaningful conversations about faith and how to put their beliefs into action.

After praying for them and saying good night, Emma and Montgomery walked to her room. Aurora and Diane sat on her couch, with an open laptop before them on the coffee table. A mostly empty bowl of popcorn sat between them.

Aurora shut the lid of her laptop. "Our movie finished half an hour ago, and we've been talking."

"I want to hear how your day went." Emma's gaze bounced between Aurora and Diane.

Diane looked at Aurora. "You first."

"I had a great day," Aurora said. "The crew is

ready to begin work on the lower level of the priests' quarters on Monday. We moved all the priests we could to the upper level, and the last few will move into the Palace once the donors leave."

"Does that mean you're finished with the dorms?" Emma asked.

Aurora chuckled. "Far from it, but this crew's part on it is done. So they'll move on to the priests' quarters."

"That's exciting," Emma said.

"But Diane's news is even more exciting," Aurora said.

Emma shifted her gaze to Diane.

"Thanks to your friends' help, we got everything moved today. Hector's new house is amazing. I helped Chloe get settled in her room and spent some time talking with Hector. We have a long way to go, and that mostly falls to me—since I'm the one who caused this whole mess."

"Be patient and trust the Sovereign," Emma said.

"But the best news is that the house has a fourth bedroom! Providing I stay out of his way and don't do something stupid, Hector said I can stay there to be closer to Chloe. I'll move there after Sunday's service."

"That's great," Emma said. "But what will you do during the day when everyone is gone?"

"I'll come here with Gabe and Chloe each day. When I'm not meeting with Olivia or studying the Holy Text, I'll spend the rest of my time working in the communication center. I feel I belong there. It's the perfect place for me."

20

PHILANTHROPY

On Sunday morning, Emma ate an early breakfast with the donors—at least those who hadn't slept in. She urged them to go to one of the three services at the ancient Temple, and then to pick one of the other services after that.

For her part, Emma's role in the services was again minor. She'd give the welcome at each of the three services in the Temple. For the other three services, she'd give the benediction—which she planned to sing.

After the final service, she met with the donors for their last meal in the cafeteria before they left.

They had been asking about Joshua, interested

in meeting him. He sat at a different table with his family and hers. She waved for him to come over.

As he approached, she reached her hand toward his. Their fingers met and intertwined. "Everyone, this is Joshua." Emma's face beamed. "And Joshua, this is everyone." With a wink, she gave a sweeping gesture to the entire group.

They all greeted him. "Thank you for sharing her with us yesterday," Harold's wife said. Then she looked at Emma. "Why don't you go eat with your family? We'll be fine. But if you have time, please stop by before you leave."

Emma really wanted to spend time with her family, but she wasn't sure if she should. "Seriously? You're okay with that?"

Everyone nodded.

"You gave so much to us yesterday," the woman said. "Now it's your turn."

"Thank you." Emma and Joshua left to enjoy lunch with each other and their families.

Forty-five minutes later, Emma returned to the donors' table. "This week was a real learning experience for me. I know we made a lot of mistakes to start with. But I think we ended well. Next year we'll do better."

"Regarding that," Harold said, "we've been

talking about all we've learned from you. That the Sovereign has blessed us so we can bless others. We have a renewed interest in how we use the money the Lord has given us. Though we've known each other for years through these annual meetings, this is the first time we've actually connected with each other—thanks to you."

"I had little to do with it," Emma said. "I just tried to do what the Sovereign told me."

"Your humility and your faith in action are two of the things that draw us to you," Harold said. "We're going to stay connected throughout the year to encourage one another in how we give and what we give to. Though we don't expect another banquet next year, it would be nice if we could reconvene and spend a Saturday with you. It's just a thought."

"It's a great thought," Emma said. "I like it. Let's make it happen." She lifted both hands toward them and blessed them.

Waving goodbye as she left, Emma and Montgomery hustled to the front of the High Priest's residence to meet Gabe so he could drive her to visit Barney.

But Gabe wasn't waiting for her. Fred was. She *so* did not want to see him. Not today. Not after what he had done last night. She needed time to process all that had happened before she could move toward reconciliation. She wasn't ready for that. Not yet.

But whether she wanted to or not, whether she was ready to or not, it was going to happen. *Help me, Sovereign*, she prayed silently.

Despite her frustration with all that Fred had done and how he had acted, Emma now realized she had made mistakes too. She had disrespected his plans and repeatedly ignored his instructions. She needed to take the first step and apologize.

Emma opened the back door of the car for Montgomery. He jumped in. Then she climbed into the front, next to Fred. Turning to him, she opened her mouth to apologize, but he held up his hand to stop her.

"I'm ashamed of my behavior for the past couple of days, especially Friday night," Fred said. "Please forgive me. I thought that the success of the fundraiser was on my shoulders, that it was up to me to secure their pledges. I never even thought to pray about it. And I didn't give you space to listen to the Sovereign for direction. Thankfully, you did what our Lord told you to do and ignored me. I apologize for getting in your way and nearly messing things up."

Emma reframed her apology. "I wasn't as supportive of you as I should've been. I'm sorry for not wanting to practice my presentation when you asked. And I'm sorry I didn't help you plan. I let you carry the entire load. Please forgive me too."

"Don't give it another thought," Fred said. "You were in the right. I was in the wrong."

"Let's put this behind us so we can move on," Emma said.

"Did you hear the final pledge numbers?" Fred asked.

"I did," Emma said. "Who would've guessed?"

"Certainly not me." Fred shook his head. "My hope was that they would continue to donate at their current levels, but the total nearly doubled."

Emma glowed. "By the way, I got my provisional license. Can I drive?"

Fred stroked his beard. "Let me think about it. Maybe on the way back." He started the car and drove toward the prison.

"With all our focus on the VIP Donor Club, we haven't had time to talk about the capital," Emma said. "How did things go after Michael and I left?"

"It was most amazing," Fred said. "I spent all

Tuesday with Ms. Cartwright, along with several members of her team. The bottom line is that we're ready to begin. We can start just as soon as we sign the papers."

"That's amazing," Emma said. "But I'm sure there's more to the story. Details. Give me details."

"Ms. Cartwright and her husband dreamed of having a venue in the capital for concerts and large meetings. They purchased property, demolished old buildings, and built a grand auditorium. But the day it passed its final inspection, her husband suffered a fatal heart attack."

Emma gasped. "That's terrible."

Fred nodded. "After that, she lost all interest in the building and was going to sell it on the day we met her. Though she didn't have peace about the buyers, she just wanted to be done with it. When they canceled, she took that as a sign from the Sovereign not to sell to them. When she met you, she took that as confirmation from the Sovereign to provide it to us for our Sunday services."

"How much does she want for it?" Emma asked.

"She didn't say. It's worth millions, but she wants to give it to us. She'll even pay for our first year's operational costs."

"What do we need to do to get it ready?" Emma asked. "How big is it?"

"The main auditorium seats 1,500. There are also three smaller meeting rooms. Opening the partitions between them will provide a bigger space for mid-sized events. There are also some offices and living quarters that the other priests and I can use. The good news is that it's ready to go. No renovations required."

"What will we do with all that space during the week?" Emma asked. "It bugs me to have a huge building that's only used a couple of hours on Sunday."

"We can rent it out during the week. There's a tremendous need for a large venue in the capital. The demand is there. We just need to tap into it."

Emma thought of her meeting with Ms. Cartwright, the woman's faith journey, and losing her husband. "Let's honor the Cartwrights and call it the Cartwright Community Center."

21

THE EMAIL

Fred, Emma, and Montgomery walked into the visitor waiting area of the prison. The regular woman wasn't there. Emma hoped this was because it was her day off. Instead, a kind-looking, older gentleman sat at the counter. He didn't seem surprised to see them. "Are you here to see Barney Clark?"

Confused, Emma walked over to the sign-in sheet. "I am."

"I really enjoy hearing you sing the doxology," the man said. He tilted his head toward his computer. "Don't tell anyone, but I watched the service online today."

Emma wasn't sure if she should be happy that

he watched or disappointed that he did so when he was supposed to be working. "I enjoy singing."

"You have a beautiful voice," the man said. "Do you want to take your dog in with you?"

"I didn't think you permitted pets," Emma said.

"I'm happy to make an exception for you. It's a slow day. No one will know."

Again, Emma wasn't sure if she should be happy for the man's generosity or disappointed that he was breaking the rules for her sake. "If it's not too much trouble, that would be great."

Minutes later, Emma walked into the secure visitor's area. She sat in the middle chair. Emma gave her thigh two quick slaps, and Montgomery leapt onto her lap. His head turned to take in the whole place. It was new to him, and he seemed excited.

A guard ushered Barney into the room and then left. Barney smiled at Emma as he sat. He picked up the handset. That's when he noticed Montgomery. "Seeing you today is even more special knowing that you went to the trouble to bring Montgomery to me. I'm honored."

Barney placed his hand on the glass that separated them. "Oh, Montgomery, how I've missed you." The puppy leapt forward to reach his former owner but smacked the glass with a thud.

Emma moved the receiver from her ear to the puppy's. She knew Barney was talking to Montgomery, but she couldn't read lips. After a while, a bored Montgomery returned to Emma's lap. He snuggled down and closed his eyes.

Barney sighed. "You were right, Emma. Seeing me confused him. And knowing that he's moved on fills me with sadness."

"But now you can move on too."

"He is now your dog," Barney said. "I must accept that."

"I doubt they'll let me bring him back anyway."

"I've been thinking a lot about our last conversation," Barney said. "Your program at the Lakeview County facility seems perfect for me. But even if I can't take part, I want to do what I can to make a positive difference here for the Sovereign. I don't know what that will look like, but I pray clarity will emerge as I read the Holy Text."

"Either way," Emma said, "I want to help you make that difference. I can see you've changed— even since our last visit. You seem . . . well, you seem happy."

"I am. It's strange to say, but ending up here is

the best thing that could've happened to me. I was so blinded by my pain and anger that I couldn't see straight, and I made so many mistakes. But you helped me get back on track. You showed me my errors and enabled me to reconnect with the Sovereign. For the first time in my life, I enjoy reading the Holy Text. And what I read finally makes sense."

"The Sovereign is clearly at work in your life," Emma said. "I pray your faith continues to grow, and that you'll have others to help."

"Since I'll never live in it again," Barney said, "I want to give you my house."

Emma shook her head.

"I thought that would be your reaction. But if you and Joshua get married, you could live there."

"It will be a few years before Joshua and I get married. The house would just sit empty."

"You're a resourceful girl—a resourceful young woman. I'm sure that between you and the Sovereign, you'll come up with a good use for it until then."

Emma still didn't feel right about it. Though she couldn't see herself ever living in it, maybe it could be used for temporary housing for people in transition. Or perhaps a halfway house.

"At least look at it. Take Joshua with you. I know that marriage is a few years away and children would be even longer, but do check out the nursery. Em and I spared no expense on it. It's filled with custom-made wooden furniture and not the cheap plastic kind. We also have two closets filled with clothes. One for a boy and the other for a girl."

"You said you were having a girl."

"We bought the clothes before we knew. They're classic designs that don't go out of style. I would be so honored to know that your children might wear them."

A shudder went through Emma. "This is a lot to take in. I'm only fifteen and still in high school, but you're talking about my wedding and me having children."

"I didn't intend to cause you angst. I guess I have too much time on my hands to think. Just know that the house, the nursery, and all its contents are available for you whenever you need it—whether you have a boy, a girl . . . or twins."

The thought of twins shook Emma, but she shrugged it off. "Twins do run in my family."

"I didn't mean to shock you," Barney said. "I just want to do what I can to provide for you and your family when the time comes."

"This is a lot to wrap my mind around," Emma said, "but thank you."

"I do have one request, however, of a more pressing nature," Barney said. "Will you reach out to Patrice—the former Prime Minister—and guide her in confessing her sins and giving her life over to the Sovereign? Then help her receive the Divine Spirit, like you did for me."

"I've tried contacting her but failed," Emma said.

"Me too," Barney said. "My letters are all returned unopened. I hope you can get through to her."

"I tried twice to meet with her in person, but she refused. I also sent her a letter that was returned. I even reached out to her in the spiritual realm. She wants nothing to do with me."

Barney sighed. "I guess that's it. There's nothing left we can do."

Emma shook her head. "We can pray."

Barney's face lit up.

"Sovereign Lord," Emma prayed, "please open Patrice's heart to receive you, trusting you in faith to save her. Please reveal to us anything we should do. Amen."

Saying goodbye, Emma and Montgomery left.

She met Fred in the waiting room, and they headed to the car. She raced to the driver's side and jumped in.

But before Emma buckled her seatbelt, she pulled out her phone to see what she had missed during her meeting with Barney. There were no texts, but an email awaited her. It was from Beatrice. "I thought you'd like to know that a letter arrived for you from Patrice Overton."

If you enjoyed *Restoring the Repentant,* please leave a review online. Your review will help others learn about this book and encourage them to read it too.

Thank you.

WHAT'S NEXT?

This concludes the nine-book story arc I planned for The Next High Priest Series. Yet that doesn't have to be the end. If you want more, that could happen. Let me know.

The series didn't resolve everything. Like me, you may have questions:

- Will Emma and Joshua stay together? Will they get married?
- Are twins in Emma's future?
- What will Emma do with Barney's house?
- Who will be the next Prime Minister? Will that person oppose Emma, or will they work together?

- How will the Sunday services go in the capital? Will Fred be able to influence the politicians?
- Will the reconfigured prison in Lakeview County accomplish what Emma envisions?
- Will Barney be accepted into the program?
- How long will Emma be High Priestess?
- Above all, will Emma's faith continue to grow?

As you think about these questions, turn the page to check out a sample from my next book, *The Curious Gift*, a contemporary young adult novella with a hint of the supernatural.

THE CURIOUS GIFT
CHAPTER 1: EIGHTEEN

It was a weepy day for Madison Monroe. In fact, it was a weepy Christmas vacation. The two-week break from school totally sucked. On the last day of school, Gram had a serious stroke. The next day she died, and they buried her two days before Christmas. Gram was her favorite person in the whole world. Not having her around anymore left a gaping hole in Madison's heart.

Her family went through the motions of Christmas: church, gifts, and a holiday feast. When Madison set the table, she included a place for Gram without thinking.

Mom swallowed hard and then forced a weak smile. "Having a place for her is a great idea.

Though she won't be with us in person, I'm sure she'll be with us in spirit."

Madison's eyes bugged out in wide-eyed horror. It weirded her out to act like Gram would be there when she wouldn't. Or would she? Death and the hope of life after death confused her. It wasn't logical, but somehow it seemed right. On her next birthday, she would turn eighteen. Maybe once she became an adult, death and stuff would begin to make sense. She hoped so.

The one thing she did know for sure was that Gram's death would ruin the rest of her senior year. *Why did you have to die and leave me all alone?* The carefree, live-for-the-moment girl had died with Gram. Gram had been in great health, with decades left, or so it seemed. Madison now realized that life could end at any moment.

Until this happened, Madison had never thought much about death. What if today were her last? *Seize the moment, Maddy girl!* When she died, she wanted to go with no regrets. Such morbid thoughts for a teenager.

After Christmas came the sucky task of going through Gram's stuff. The process was simple. Decide what to throw away, what to give away, and what to keep. Today, Madison handled the kitchen, while Mom went through Gram's personal stuff.

Madison held a flour sifter in her hands, pondering which pile to put it in. Though Mom didn't even own one, Gram used the sifter whenever she baked. Often Madison would help, especially when it was time to make Gram's special holiday biscuits—using her top-secret recipe. But this Christmas dinner had had no biscuits. The recipe had died with Gram, since she hadn't written it down and refused to tell anyone. "There'll be time for that later."

Madison inhaled slowly, trying to hold back her tears. "Keep it or donate it?"

"What, Honey?"

Madison spun around. There stood Mom. With an ashen face, silent tears rolled down her mother's cheeks. Her hands cradled a wrapped gift. "It's . . . for you." Trembling, Mom extended the package to Madison.

"What?" Before her stroke, Gram had bought, wrapped, and delivered the family's Christmas gifts. "We opened them all on Christmas." Madison shook her head slowly in shock.

"It says, 'Happy Birthday, Madison.'"

"My birthday isn't for two months."

"It seems she planned ahead." Mom extended the package to Madison.

"I guess this goes in the pile of things we keep." Madison's attempt at humor failed. She knew this as soon as a flurry of Mom's tears unleashed. It wasn't long before Madison joined in. They ended up in a tangled heap on the couch, shoulders heaving as they wept in each other's arms.

When they were too spent to cry anymore, they just sat there. Madison didn't need a mirror to know she looked like one hot mess. A quick glance at Mom's face was all she needed to know what hers looked like.

"Good thing your father's not here. He never has learned how to handle our tears." They shared a much-needed mother-daughter laugh. Then Mom placed the gift on Madison's lap.

"Should I wait until my birthday or open it now?"

"What do you want to do?"

"I don't know." Madison shook her head in slo-mo indecision. "Part of me thinks I should wait, and part of me thinks opening it now might help with the mourning process." Then she shrugged. "Whatever that means."

"I think your grandmother would be fine with

either decision. In her eyes, you could do no wrong."

That brought another wave of tears to Madison. "I think I'll wait." Then she wavered. "What if I open the card now and the gift on my birthday?"

"That would be lovely."

Though Madison usually ripped open envelopes, this time she moved with deliberate slowness. This would be the last card she'd ever open from Gram. She skipped the verse on the inside and went straight to Gram's handwritten note. "This is my most treasured possession, and it changed my life. I want you to have it. Much love always, Gram."

"Oh, Mom! There's no way I can wait. I have to open it now."

"I agree," Mom said. "Would you like some privacy?"

"Stay," Madison begged. This time she tore into the package, ripping at the paper to discover its contents. Though Madison didn't know what to expect, what she saw surprised her. It was a book. An old, old book with a worn leather cover. In fancy gold-embossed script the title said, *How to Make a Difference in the Lives of Other People.*

"I've never seen this book before." Madison glanced at her mom with questioning eyes. "Yet she says it's her most prized possession."

"I've never seen it either." Mom shook her head.

In eager expectation, Madison fanned through the pages. Each page was blank. Every one. Not a single word on a single page.

Read more in Peter's upcoming book, *The Curious Gift*, due out in 2026.

ABOUT PETER DEHAAN

Peter DeHaan is an adult who dreams of being a teenager. When he's not contemplating grown-up thoughts, his mind retreats to the domain of invented worlds with his loyal and most real, yet still imaginary, friends. What grand adventures they have: righting wrongs, solving problems, and making their world a better place to live.

His first published adventures come to life in "The Next High Priest Series"—a faith-friendly speculative fiction adventure in a world just like ours . . . only different.

Next up is *The Curious Gift*, a YA contemporary novella with a hint of the supernatural.

Then comes "The Ice Creamed Series," a present-day quest for friendship and love, all the while trying to survive high school unscathed and ping-ponging between responsible impulses and irresponsible slipups.

Want more? Get a free short-story prequel about Emma along with news of upcoming books when you sign up to receive updates at PeterDeHaan.com/fiction.

FICTION BOOKS BY PETER DEHAAN

The Next High Priest Series

Seeking the Sovereign

Confronting the Chaos

Dueling the Devil

Reforming the Religion

Freeing the Prisoners

Fighting the Fanatics

Perfecting the Priesthood

Pursuing the Politicians

Restoring the Repentant

Learn more at PeterDeHaan.com/fiction.